Emory James Haynes

A Farm-House Cobweb

A Novel

Emory James Haynes

A Farm-House Cobweb
A Novel

ISBN/EAN: 9783337349097

Printed in Europe, USA, Canada, Australia, Japan

Cover: Foto ©Andreas Hilbeck / pixelio.de

More available books at **www.hansebooks.com**

A FARM-HOUSE COBWEB

A Novel

BY

EMORY J. HAYNES

NEW YORK
HARPER & BROTHERS PUBLISHERS
1895

TO

MY FRIEND

JOHN S. HUYLER

A FARM-HOUSE COBWEB

WE held our singing-schools that winter in the town-hall. For two or three seasons previous Northbrook had been fairly sprinkled over with smaller schools in different parts of the town. As many as four different teachers had gathered small companies, singing their do, re, mes in the North District, at the Meadows, at East Brook, and at Mechanicsville.

Old Philander Pepper, that veteran, had led in our parts generally. The venerable man had been teaching our grandfathers and grandmothers to sing, up and down the stony hill-sides and vales of Vermont, long before we were born. He was a most worthy gentleman, Philander P., whose voice was now, however, like a scythe much ground, with its thin back and a feathery edge.

But when this young Dartmouth student fairly began to compete with him by getting up a class in the Centre Village, poor Philander lost popu-

1

larity rapidly. In fact all the four other schools
in our township were to be consolidated this winter of 18— at the Centre Village, using the great
,room of the town-hall, as I have said.

This handsome, graceful, popular young teacher's name was Arthur Alfred Felton. Mine is
plain Elisha Stone. You see them for the first
time together on this printed page. So I used to
write them side by side years ago, and then fall
to studying them long and with many a heartache. As I sat by my solitary wood grate in my
farm-house often I wrote them by fancy in the
flicker of the firelight, when the candle had burned
out. His name looks the best, I am bound to
confess.

I used to wonder if Mary Holyoke ever wrote
those two names together and studied them as I
did. She was poetess enough to make their two
owners dance in the mimic quadrilles of glowing
embers in the ample fireplace of her father's library. Yes, quite likely she did this. Would to
God she had done no more than that with his
name, with his shape in her maiden visions of to-
morrow !

"Will you go to—allow me to escort you to
the singing-school this winter?" I had asked
Mary Holyoke along in November.

I remember that I drove my colt Skip up
there that day and halted in front of her father's
door. As I could not leave the colt, Mary came
round from the back stoop, where she was en-

gaged rinsing off the milk-pails just after straining, to speak with me. Her sleeves were rolled to
her dimpled elbows, notwithstanding the frosty air.

What a picture of graceful health she was!
No doubt I was as nervous as my colt, yet I had
an honest and sober purpose in my heart. I loved
the girl then. I had loved that child ever since
she was born. I was ten years her senior. I had
worked as chore-boy on her wealthy father's farm
the very summer she was born. Now, however,
I owned a fine farm of my own, small but as
good land, if I do say it, as ever lay out-of-doors.
I had seen her grow up, and I had waited. When
her father sent her to Montpelier to school I
bought a few books, and I read and studied in
secret while I waited. I tried to keep up with
what I imagined she was doing. I carefully
measured her attainments as I saw her return,
vacation after vacation, more and more a lady.
Working all day in the fields, and over books at
night, would have broken me down had I been
less vigorous. I tried to believe that my vigorous health and rugged appearance blotted out
the ten years difference between us. I think so
still. Maybe I am of a sober vein mentally ; but
I must be allowed to confess that my hopes, my
spirits, my generosity of intent, keep me young.
There never was a boy in our district who could
get me off my feet at snap-the-whip.

"Whoa! will you?" I said, as the mare kept
dancing.

Then Mary came up and put her small hand
on the tire of my wheel, replying to my invitation : "I have subscribed myself this year, but
I will be glad to accompany you occasionally."

Indeed ! Was it so ? The season before Mary
had gone in my sleigh to Philander Pepper's
school at East Brook school-house all the Thursday evenings of the course. This season, however, she had sent her father down to subscribe
for the class in the village herself, had she ? I
ought to have taken warning then, though I do
not think I really did.

"The first night then, Mary," I answered.
"Let me take you the first night. It's going to
be a big school ; we shall have a crowd of sleighs
thronging and bothering at the door after the
class breaks up, and your father is getting along
in years."

"Certainly," she had said ; and we chatted a
few words more, when I drove away. I might
have put the mare in the barn and spent the
evening, but I did not. Still we parted in smiles.
What a smile that young creature had, as she
stood there, artless, gracious, serving her home
with a domestic fidelity so different from the
haughty contempt for work that characterizes
young girls of her station. She was like some
queen in Macaulay of which I had read. Her
eyes had a beauty of blue that Byron had never
sung in all my reading. She was as good as she
was beautiful, and that's a fact !

The singing-school—let me get at the description of it. I can see the old hall yet—on the hill, just beyond the Congregational church. We used the horse-sheds at the back of the church for our teams. That was square with the Lord, for we all sang in the choir. The building was high-lodged, overlooking all the village roofs. The two rows of windows were blazing with the warm light that was laying itself out in rosy tints on the snowy earth of the village green. The new moon hung out, I remember, low down towards her setting over South Mountain, sharp as a harvest sickle. The air was so clear, the night so blue-dark, that the copper of the moon's shadowed part was plainly to be seen, making a curious orb of two colors.

How the stars used to laugh in those fond heavens, and seemed in that cold rare air to be so stuck upon the surface of the sky that one could pluck them off with a long apple-picker.

Here was the union store on the left, there on the right the new tavern, the lamps from their windows flashing in lanes of light that met in the centre of the street by the town pump. Some of the boys watered their colts at the frost-rimmed log trough, but I did not; my mare was too warm.

I can see them yet — those shapely Vermont Morgans, steaming with their exertion, proudly jingling their bells, which in those days they wore as a shining circlet around the body. What a

procession of us winding up meeting-house hill!
The snow was two feet deep, if one floundered
out of the path; therefore every fellow in line.

"Hollo, Zeek! That you? Catch him, hi!"
The cry of warning was passed along from a doz-
en mouths. Luckily Ezekiel Blood had left Lucy
Tennant at the door.

There was a bit of excitement as the foolhardy
Zeek had tried to turn out in the deep snow, getting a tip-over. He would have been wiser had
he followed us more sedate mortals on that half
sweep round to the horse-sheds. However, the
colt behaved beautifully, and stopped, all like a
frightened deer, as two or three shouted to her.
Poor Ezekiel, as he rises before me a Santa Claus
of memory, tugging after the trembling creature,
robes on his shoulder, and that precious new whip
in his hand. "That was a Boston - bought whip,"
he said. Ah me, that happy night! Ezekiel died
in the wars two years later.

One by one we filed under the lamp which hung
in its iron-bound cage above the door, each sleigh-
load of rosy girls and stalwart boys. There was
no gaudy awning to hide coy beauties from the
peeping moon. There was no lounging officer to
impede their springing flight up the steps, as I
see in cities before the opera. The winds played
with their wraps, buffeting their silvery voices
after our retreating sleighs.

"Good - evening, Hannah." This was Hannah
Castlereigh.

"Do tell, Marinda! I thought you were visiting in Boston. Rather be here, had you not, my dear?" This was Marinda Joslyn. I knew all their sweet voices; our "set."

"Indeed we would, my dears," I heard Cynthia Littlewood cry, shaking the snow-flakes from her musk-rat furs. Cynthia's fellow was Horace Parkridge, from the North District, and never was a more daring horseman or a more perfect jehu of a driver than "Hod," as we called him. There never was a Horace, by-the-way, in all Vermont or New Hampshire who got the use of his whole name or escaped being called "Hod." The boy had driven so fast those ten miles that Cynthia was sprinkled all over her shapely shoulders with crystal frost, and even in her black and shining hair it shone, as in later years I have seen diamond dust sparkling in the tresses of society women at stately receptions.

Can I not hear them yet? The broad entry-way full of charming women, stamping their stout little boots free of the snow, cooing like a flock of pigeons the latest bits of neighborly gossip, while they waited for us boys till we picked out each his own to escort her up the stairs. We made a good roomful, nigh two hundred of us, all seated and ready to start on a pitch.

"I shall begin at once," said Felton, almost as soon as we were seated, "with a preliminary separation and location of the four parts. Basses on my left, in the wing seats, please. Promptly, gentlemen. Tenors take the right; altos here; sopranos here. I see you have done all this before, anticipating me." He stepped down gingerly from the platform to the floor with stick in hand.

We expected this rearranging to suit himself, of course, but rather later in the evening. He was, however, as prompt as a colonel of volunteers. I had planned it all at my own solitary fireside evening on evening as I sat looking at the shadows and flashings of the fire-log. Since I sung bass and Mary Holyoke sung soprano, there was no good reason why we should not be located side by side. Do you not see? Mary could be the last one on a seat full of sopranos and I the first one of a seat full of basses. I felt sure she was among "the leading voices" that would be there. I was forced to reckon myself nearer a leading bass than I really was, no doubt, plotting my desired place. Except for Arthur Alfred Felton, she would never have thought of objecting to my plan. She was never more cordial and gracious to me than on that night, from the time I took her up at her father's horse-block till we were seated in that row; so there, if I do say so!

"Let us try ' Federal Street,' " began the master, "and get our voices in trim."

The majestic old melody moved off at once, noble as a march of an army with banners. Two hundred good voices there were, mostly youthful, though gray-haired men, not many women gray-haired, were here and there in the throng.

Old Deacon Landers had sung in our choirs among the tenors for fifty years. Whether his kind blue eyes looked through his spectacles on the page or over it always puzzled us to tell. The deacon and his life-long friend 'Kiah Lowrey, always together in every singing-school since I could remember, sat side by side. And why not? For they knew more than any master whom we ever had, 'Kiah being expert with the bass viol and the deacon the church chorister of thirty years. These two of heavy foot; each would insist always in beating time with the boot.

The deacon, moreover, relied upon his tuning-fork to catch the pitch even after we had the piano. "Twang-hum-do, re, me." But as both these gentlemen were among the wealthiest farmers in our parts, and always heavy subscribers to new music, to the oyster supper at the end of the term, and present of a new baton to the master, what mattered about their old-fashioned way?

"'Hebron!'" cried Arthur Alfred Felton, in his rich deep tone. "And now, as we come to that natural in the upper staff, ladies, do not be afraid of it!"

We start, we are rapped to silence, we get further explanation. We get agoing on "Hebron" at last to suit his exacting ear.

But he was handsome though, as he stood forth there dressed in city-cut garments, six feet tall,

broad-shouldered, black and wavy hair, low wide
brow, hazel eyes, a side-whisker sweeping long
and low for one so young, and exposing his full
lips free to use their smiles. And manly, too, one
might confess. It was a frank, honest air he wore
at least. He made friends even among men. The
small boys liked him, and kept silence in the side
settees at his slightest request. As a rule, our
singing teachers had no end of trouble with the
boys, often ejecting them, scolded at the whispering spectators, and not unfrequently ended up
with unpopular orders that " no spectators should
be admitted," expect the village minister, the
judge, and a few dignitaries.

But there was a spell in Arthur Alfred Fen-
ton's slightest request. " Let us have attention.
We are glad to welcome our friends, but they will
see the necessity of silence." That was enough.

Were you ever at a country singing - school
when the vital air without was twenty degrees
below zero ? When the boreal light, arching
the sky, made each singing mortal thrice vital ?
When, within, the huge box-stove, throbbing red,
fought with the chill till the windows were cov-
ered with steam, and faces of man and maid flushed
high ? When, with each added tune, the heart
beat quicker as the music grew in grace ? Majestic song ! A world of it, in the outer air, in the
room, in our hearts. Mighty words, the hymns
of the ages, the aspirant prayers of saints, full of
praise and promise, life, death, sorrow, joy, and

the immortal life. Not a solitary ditty, not a
line of doggerel, but great swelling numbers of
the soul's best wish towards God.

Who, who could go through two hours of it,
and not be a better man therefor? We laughed,
of course, and between times chatted small talk,
passed candy to the girls, and cast sheep's-eyes.
But, for all that, we were exalted. It was a strange
commingling of heavenly and earthly emotions.

May Heaven forgive me if I did a sacrilegious
thing; but, after all those years of waiting, then
at last, my very soul amid the clouds, I brought
myself to the point of the momentous question.
We were singing Anna Barbauld's hymn to the
tune "Zephyr," from Bradbury's new book. The
first stanza ran,

> "How blest the sacred tie that binds,
> In union sweet, according minds."

As we paused at the end of the line I could not
say that I turned my head upon my shoulders to
look directly at Mary; but I was conscious of
some subtle, psychic perception—I think that's
the word—that told me that she was instinct with
the apt meaning of the couplet. A smile stole
over her dear face; it parted her trembling lips
till the white pearl showed their two full rows;
and as the air climbed upward on the opening of
the last couplet,

> "How swift the heavenly course they run,
> Whose hearts, whose faith, whose hopes are one,"

she turned and looked on me. I was nearly overwhelmed! As I am writing these annals for no
eyes but my own and those of my most intimate
friends, I need not be ashamed to confess my emotion. I remember fearing Arthur Alfred Felton's
rap to order over some error in execution ; fearing some wicked halt, a chiding that would compel us to forego the next stanza, when there would
be a silent, an awkward pause. What, then, should
I say to Mary? how should I act? But, no, it was
correctly sung; Arthur Alfred smiled, nodded,
bent forward with his whole body, struck up and
down the two-two time ; we swept on, as a fairy
cloud in summer gales, over skies of blue ; on, on
went the melody, bearing upward the next stanza :

"To each the soul of each how dear,
What jealous love, what holy fear,
How doth the generous flame within
Refine from earth and cleanse from sin."

As I recall it all, after the flight of years, in my
ecstasy I drop the pen and seat myself to touch
again the piano to the tune "Zephyr." The re-
production is complete! I live it all over again.
Would any chance kinsman, reading this history, understand me fully, let him either sing or
play or imagine the old and stately numbers of
that tune, freight the harmony with Miss Barbauld's words, and so catch the other meaning
that they had to our young hearts. Else he
may judge me foolishly profane.

"Last stanza!" shouted Arthur Alfred, with a
stamp of his foot and features illumed with de-
light.

> "Nor shall the glowing flame expire
> When Nature droops her sickening fire;
> Then shall they meet in realms above—
> A heaven of joy, because of love."

"That was fine; we are doing gloriously!"
cried the master. "Ten minutes' recess."

I turned my eyes fully now on the sweet face at
my side. Surely none of the dark shadows that
have since intervened between that face and me,
no threatenings of the tragedies that have since
clouded it from my view, were visible then. We
two did not, for a brief moment, rise, as others
were doing, in happy confusion, all about us.
Strange to say, our hands were clasped, and we
knew it not. It seemed a happy eternity, those
mere instants of time that we sat there, till suddenly we were interrupted by the master approaching.

"Good-evening. Miss Holyoke, I believe?"
Mary snatched her hand free from mine, and
sprung to her feet blushing. God help me to
believe that he had not detected our hands
clasped. I want to think as well of him as I can.
Heaven knows that he is in much need of char-
ity, wherever in the universe he wanders. No!
He had but rarely met me before, for I had only
occasionally attended upon his school, being a

pupil of Pepper's the preceding season. I have
recorded, however, that I frequently left Mary
Holyoke at his school at East Brook district
school-house. He must have known that.

"Mr. Felton!" murmured Mary, in recognition; but really she gave him no further welcome than any lady might properly have accord-
ed a comparative stranger. I am sure of that,
am I not? God help me, I cannot tell! I have
thought of this so much that at times my memory seems like a fire burning in the woods, as I
have seen it in late October, turning everything
into little black scrolls or heaps of ashes. The
man did not address me, surely. Mary noticed
this, and attempted, like a true lady, to insist
upon an introduction.

"This is our neighbor—"

"Miss Holyoke," he persisted, "you must sit
here on the left of the main aisle after recess.
Really, your voice is as sweet as—" But he did
not quite dare to finish his soft compliment.
There was something in her aspect that made
him pause. I could have told him that that was
not the way, by bold assault, to approach her
heart. On the pause she pulled me in again.

"Our neighbor, Mr. Elisha Stone, Mr. Felton."

He turned a sharp glance on me, which was yet
not rude, and tossed to me.

"Glad to know you, Mr. Stone. Let's see; you
are a bass voice, I believe. Gentlemen turn out
pretty well at this school, better than in most in-

stances. The ladies are usually in the large majority. Reside in this district, Mr. Stone?"

Yet all the while, had it been written on his brow, I could have read it no more plainly that he was measuring me, and I now believe had been thinking about me, at the side of this bright lady, for the last hour. I felt it all now. Of course he had. He had certainly marked her presence, with inward satisfaction, from the very first moment of calling the school to order. He had resolved to make much of the little previous acquaintance with her promptly on recess. No wonder at that, for she was the fairest in the room—a fine voice and a rich man's daughter. Had he not instantly stepped down from the platform to take her hand? Had he not brushed by the committee, who even now were standing at his back, awaiting him with some important business of this first night of the school?

Still I was not a fool, but a patient, strong man; confident, too, after my many years waiting by my faith in her. That is, almost confident, I say. We had not actually spoken the word; no, no, that is true; let me do them both justice. It was only the music and hymn that had spoken.

"The school supplies a social want in a rural community," I answered, taking up the idea expressed by him, and we shook hands. "We shall have a fine winter with you, I trust, Mr. Felton."

He did not respond to me; I would not like to say that he ignored me, but he dropped my hand, placed his own two hands wide apart, on the back of the settee in front of us, and wearing a charm in his fine face, which came like a flash of the sunrise the moment his eyes turned to hers, he resumed :

"We shall certainly expect you, Miss Holyoke, to allow us your leadership. Nature has gifted you; and in many ways—pardon me. I shall not take no for an answer ! On the main aisle, please, after recess. Remember that I am master here," he rounded up, laughing playfully, "and my word is law."

"You certainly must excuse me."

"Nothing of the kind," he answered. "Now that is settled—first of the sopranos."

"But Miss Cynthia Littlewood had that post of honor in your school at this hall last season. I am a new-comer. See, Miss Littlewood is watching us now with a jealous eye. She has sat at the first place all this evening. Did you not put her there ?"

Arthur Alfred Felton turned to look. A thoughtful, puzzled expression thickened on his face. It was all a matter of last winter's history. I confess I knew very little about it. He was reviewing it all in that one moment as he looked at Cynthia Littlewood. There stood the girl, twenty feet away, tall, black and glossy hair, complexion of marble, dark eyes, flashing one moment and softening the next, regarding us.

Horace Parkridge, her escort, was in vain talk-

ing to her pretty ear that was towards him.
Here had been a history; the village had talked
of it. Some said there would yet be a tragedy.
I remember that I told "Hod" Parkridge to be-
ware; that a girl's first love was likely to burn
long, like smouldering fire in spring turf. But
the summer had followed, and the student teacher
had gone back to his months of books at the college. At the June training and the Fourth-of-
July ride that we had Cynthia had accepted
Horace's invitations. Would to heaven they had
been wed, as at one time it was supposed they
would be, at Thanksgiving!

"Ah! Miss Littlewood, indeed." And Felton put his long white forefinger to his lips; then
throwing up his hands in a fine gesture, he continued, decisively, "No, that is all right. You
are the first soprano; I want you near; I can ar-
range everything in a moment." And, shaking
both his hands in front of him deprecatingly, he
moved over to offer his first welcome of the evening to Miss Cynthia. Instantly her marble face,
at his approach, was as warm as a sunset in haying time.

CHAPTER II

"WHAT in chain lightning does the fellow want of both of them ?" growled Horace Parkridge as soon as we were called to order again and fairly seated. We had not had time to open our books before he had accosted me.

"Hush, Hod," I whispered back to him behind my raised Bradbury as he sat in the next row.

"I am leaning forward so that no one but you can hear," he fairly hissed. His breath was hot as he spoke. "Tell me what his power is that he can gain their consent like that. There is Miss Holyoke in Cynthia's place and Cynthia on the next seat in the second place as submissive as a lamb. He has tact or some wonderful power, has he not ?"

"Yes, yes, wait till some other time. Do not say anything more, Horace. I myself advised Miss Holyoke to take her place."

"Gosh! You did!"

An hour later Parkridge and I were buttoning on our buffalo coats and descending the stairs with the other men to get our teams. As we stepped into the lower hall, through the open door, it struck us full in the face—the storm.

"Here it comes, a regular mountaineer!" cried Parkridge, lowering his head.

"You at least ought not to complain of this after your winter at the north pole," I replied, catching breath.

The boy had served two years at Annapolis; but for some prank he had fallen into disgrace and our Congressman had got the poor cadet a place on Captain Kane's last polar expedition. Let's see, have I mentioned this before? I think not. And did I put it on record that he was our minister's son? Elder Parkridge was both preacher and farmer, so when Horace came home from the polar expedition, worn and starved to a skeleton, and his gentle mother had taken him again in her arms, as if he were a baby, it won the wild boy's heart anew; for his mother's sake, at any rate, he had turned farmer, and sobered down to work the old place. He might well do so, being the parson's only child. But how long he would continue in such a quiet life I had often doubted. He had almost a possession of the devil as we went down-stairs together.

"This is going to be as hard a storm as ever struck us beyond the North Cape, my neighbor," said Horace. "I know these Vermont mountains; I have predicted this for the last two days of clear weather. Did you ever see such transparent air and brilliant sunlight as we have had? That means the mischief to pay. This morning also the northern lights, as I went out to fodder the sheep, made the whole heavens luminous. Such tongues of white fire! Such rushing and snapping in the zenith, till the sheep looked up fairly frightened. I knew what such signs meant."

"Let us keep together on our way up the north road," said I, as we ducked our heads and ran for the horse-sheds.

"Certainly," he replied, while we were unhaltering. "Now look at the horses: they shake and start with fear. It is animal instinct foretelling what a night we are to have. Wish you were in your warm stable, don't you, Princess," patting his sorrel filly on the neck. "See here," the boy added, holding in his curb as a moment later we were seated in our sleighs and the horses were rearing to get off—"see here, Stone, our first duty is, of course, to get home, but I want to thank you for your invitation up to your apple-paring. I'll be there; and now I have some serious things to counsel with you about, as a shipmate. Our farms are side by side; that is, father's and yours. Now, my boy, this gentleman, Felton—"

"Not now, Hod. We want to get through this storm."

"Whoa! Yes, sir. But it is now, neighbor! In the teeth of this gale I want to speak and say what's on my heart."

"No; we are fools to wait five minutes."

"Well," he shouted, as I began to move off, "is he going to try the drive to West Village depot to-night?"

"Yes, siree!" came singing on the wind in pat reply as the gayest sleigh in all the county backed out of the shed just behind us.

"It is Felton!" I exclaimed, under my breath, pulling up my team to warn Horace against talking too loud. "Felton has a livery team from the hotel at the West Village. Quick he is. Don't catch him napping for the sake of courtesies and good-byes on such a night."

"Was he alone?" bawled Horace.

"Yes, alone to-night," the same voice cried, as its owner, having turned around, dashed away, the runners cutting the crust like the tearing of cotton cloth.

"Do you know what that hotspur will dare?" asked Horace of me.

"Try to slip across the Round Pond," I answered.

"Yes, and perish!" I caught from Horace's lips as we parted to go around to the front. There was savage exultation in his tone. Heaven forgive the boy; and a preacher's son, too! But do not lions rend each other for the sake of the mate that one of them would steal? Nothing so rouses the fierceness of a man's nature as to be crossed in a love affair.

The menacing roar of the wind gave me little time for moralizing. I soon had Mary Holyoke springing over my sleigh robe to my side.

"Can we ever face this wind?" asked Mary, as we tucked ourselves into the sleigh, snatching at the robes which the gale disputed.

"Still we must if we are ever to get home," I answered, trying to be cheerful about it, but I now record here that in all my life I had never confronted such a whirlwind in snow.

As we were creeping along in front of the hotel through the haze I heard a voice shouting out for general information apparently and the pleasure of telling startling news : "Telegram at the post-office !—hurricane—no trains—Albany buried," and similar direful tidings as I was able to catch it through the crying of the storm. There were knots of excited villagers gathered on the steps of the hotel already, as along the sea-coast the hardy fishermen gather to watch for distressed sails.

"Who says 'telegraphic news?'" demanded a ringing voice behind me.

"Hod Parkridge, is that you?" I asked, recognizing him. "See here, old fellow, you and I simply must, on our lives, keep together up this road."

"True, 'Lish, but let's get this bulletin here. You know I have been in the government service, and something weighty has come over the wires even to our little village. Say, men, there ! Give us the latest despatch."

"'Tis a special to the *Gazette*," yelled a voice from the piazza in response.

The *Gazette* was our little village news sheet. It was made up for the most part of the record of big potatoes, weddings, and engagements, with a

precious small lot of news from the outer world.
It rarely had any telegrams, except when our village autocrat, the politician in those parts, paid
for election news. Therefore a telegram at other
times indicated a national sensation in shape of
some great calamity abroad. The officious villager waddled down to the sleigh readily enough,
partly because he wished to be obliging, and also
because, if we were to hear him at all—the little,
fat, wheezy fellow—he must come to the side of
our vehicles, and then gasped out to us the general
information that a telegram had been received
from the West Village that there were no trains
up from White River Junction since noon, there
were no Boston mails, and that a regular hurricane was stretching all the way from here to New
York, Albany, Buffalo, "and Timbuctoo," as he
said. He, moreover, went on to declare that
" 'Twas one o' them things that his boy Jack, out
West, called a bluzzard. Then he added, between
wheezes: " Better stop and put up the gals here
in town, for you never c'n get hum."

" Oh no, never !" exclaimed Mary.

" No, certainly not," put in Cynthia. "Let us
drive on. We girls are Vermonters."

" You will need to be polar bears, my dears,"
said Parkridge, thoughtfully, "to endure the
north road six or seven miles on such a night as
this. Still—"

" G'over to my house, friends," said the kind-
hearted villager, in a neighborly way. "I know

how particler folks is about talking, and no doubt
'twon't ever do for the girls to stay here away
from home."

"Oh no, no? What would father and mother do
if I didn't come home?" urged Mary. "Let's take
all the risks. We certainly can make the road.
Your colts, boys, are the best in the county."

That touch as to the colts brought the mettle
both to my arms and to Horace's, I am sure. Of
course our colts were able. In another instant
we both had reached over and just laid a touch
of the whip with the slightest caress on the flanks
of our two mares, and we were off. My colt, I
am sure, had never felt more of the lash than that
in her life, and I doubt if she ever had so much,
except upon one occasion, since she was broken.
Ah, how we sprang out into those drifts! But it
was impossible to keep that pace for five rods in
the face of the gale. It would slow down a steam-
engine.

"It is hard to breathe," gasped Mary, as she
leaned towards me behind her muff.

I threw the great black bear-skin robe clean
over her shapely head, and drew her up close to
me. It made my heart leap wilder than the colt
to be conscious of her precious self so near to my
person.

"Better walk," bawled Horace a few minutes
later from behind. The nose of his filly was
spouting steam on our shoulders, and the red skin
in her nostrils seemed bursting its blood-vessels.

The moon's full yellow light, behind this thick bank of cloud and snow, loaned to the whole weird night an ashen gray color, which was ghastly, so that it was by no means dark. It was worse than dark; it was that hobgoblin light which one only sees in storms when the moon is behind a cloud.

"No, Horace; we shall perish walking. The wind is in our backs. We certainly can try to trot," I urged; and we both speeded up a little.

"So many ghosts in the air. This is simply sublime!" whispered Mary. The girl was gamy, and kept trying to talk.

The sweep of the snow was highly exciting. One lost his consciousness of danger once in a while in watching the streamers of white that fell like handfuls of grain flying out of a sower's hand in the furrows; handfuls on handfuls of this cutting powder, as if the Almighty himself were sowing the earth—these furrowed hills and vales—with the chill of death. The cold came down on us by handfuls, colder, colder, every minute.

"I hear the roaring of the pines," murmured Mary, just below my ear. "That is two miles certainly, and only four miles more to home. But is it not fearful, the voices of the old trees?"

"If the chestnuts in among those hemlocks will only keep their precious branches to themselves, they may bellow all they please."

"Look out, there !" Horace shouted. "Heavens, see that old chestnut come down !"

"And the hemlock just behind it !" cried Cynthia's shrill voice. "God protect us ! Boys, we must not attempt to go through the woods. Turn down the left towards the lake, and we will get under the cliff."

"Right, my lady ; we have no choice, for the road is blocked," I answered. "But it is a serious question if we can turn around."

Indeed, it was no easy matter. It seemed at first simply impossible to turn back to the southwest and confront this tornado. The instant I threw my foot clear of the robe to get out, the wind stripped the bear-skin from the sleigh. There was a shower of sparks and the flash of fire. Our new-fashioned foot-stove was overturned. The lamp in it—a new-fangled patent thing not half so good as the warm soapstone or brick — had ignited the fur of the robe. The next moment the robe was three rods away on the wind, and as I leaped after it to catch it, where it had been swept into the branches of a fallen hemlock, I heard a shriek behind, and looked to see that my sleigh had been overturned.

"I have got your colt," yelled Horace, and the dear fellow had promptly sprung to save my mare.

"Can you hold the two horses?" I answered ; "I will be there in a minute." And, indeed, I was as back quickly as I could bound. I got the mare by the nose. "Now slowly, Mary. Are you hurt?"

"No; all right. Whoa!"

"Cynthia, you can rein my horse around. Easy, easy. There, hold her. Here Elisha," and Horace handed me the lines of my animal. I righted my sleigh and hung to my horse. Mary flew back to her place, and nestled under the covers. Then we began that most trying quarter of a mile of retreat along the edge of the woods—the most trying, I say, in my remembrance of any contest I ever had with nature.

"The windward of these woods is not as quiet as the lee would be," yelled Horace — he tried to be good-natured and keep up the conversation —"but it is better than the open; breaks the wind. Courage; just as soon as we get down by the cliff, even the windward of the rocks will be quite bearable."

That was true enough, as we soon experienced, but the gigantic drifts were now more appalling almost than any other object we had met upon the way. The masses of the pelting snow, hurled back from the black front of the rocks, piled at their feet so high that it was simply out of the question to attempt to keep to the highway. Far up the front of the craggy masses, on shelf and shoulder of the ledges, wreaths and festoons in fantastic shapes of white reminded me of the stories that I used to hear about these cliffs by Round Pond when I was a boy. They said the eagles made their nests there, though I had never seen an eagle in my day. In the ashen light a score of eagles seemed bending their beaks and flapping their wings, ready to swoop down upon us with some uncanny salutation.

As the gale went roaring over the tops of the cliffs it uttered peculiar cries, almost human moans, and these frightened the girls all the more, and almost cowed our hearts.

"What shall we do?" asked Mary, piteously; "perish here not four miles from home?"

"I say!" cried Horace, just then.

"Well!" I bawled back to him, at my wit's end, I confess.

"I will get out and lead your horse. You take mine by the bridle over the back of your sleigh, and I will show you Crocker's lane. We'll turn down through that and over the railroad when we come to the pond. Well—then—is your horse sharp shod?"

"Yes," I answered.

"So is Princess. Then, of course, we will be all right. We'll have a highway swept clean of the snow all the way to West Village, where we'll probably have to spend the night." And promptly the Polar explorer began his task at the head of my animal.

It was half an hour's good work to get down on the railroad, and from that to the ice, but we did it at length. Once on the surface of the lake our track was clear. A blue-black surface, transpar-

ent as still water is when frozen, lay before us,
swept as a turkey's-wing duster would sweep it.
Nothing but a calked shoe would have held on
that road. The storm pushed the sleighs at an
angle as the horses pulled them forward. The
right runner spun sideways along the track. I
was in constant apprehension of some nodule,
some roughness, or a crack. To strike that "side
on," as Horace expressed it, would be instant destruction, for we should be hurled to the icy pave-
ment with the force of a cannon-ball. However,
no such untoward event transpired, and we were
quite felicitating ourselves upon our escape when
suddenly Horace cried out:

"Look there!"

It was one of those fierce vocal sounds which a
man utters rarely in a lifetime, freighted with
terror and alarm and heart sympathy. The boy
was rising up in his sleigh and pulling at the lines
with all his might to bring Princess to a halt. I
shot to his side like a flash of light; before I could
begin to rein in, our sleighs locked at the rave,
and we slewed into the drift along the bank together, the colts in a tangle, and we stopped.

"There's Felton's sleigh—what is left of it!"
yelled Horace, pointing with his big gloved forefinger through the gloom ahead.

"Yes," I gasped; "he has caught his runner in
that crack. We narrowly escaped it. But where
is the trotter that he drove?"

"Sure enough, where?" asked Cynthia, uncov-

ering her head, her whole heart in her tone of
alarm. "And where is the teacher?"

I did not myself fancy the tone of too tender
solicitude in which the girl spoke, but the effect
on me was as nothing in comparison with its effect
on Horace Parkridge's quick ear. Still my turn
was to come. Mary Holyoke now unhooded herself to the blast, asking, in pretty trepidation:
"Boys, can we not find him? Is he?—do you? It
cannot be that he has perished in the drifts."

"What is that white mound in its winding-
sheet of snow?" asked Cynthia, her dark eyes full
of a lustre that I feared her heart inspired.

In a twinkling Horace was running ahead towards the object designated. With a few quick
strokes he uncovered it. Simultaneously a low
but piteous moan came faintly through the mist,
and I recognized it as the cry of an animal in
pain. I was prepared to hear him call out: "It is
his horse, with a broken leg."

"Almost better if it were himself," was Cynthia's plaintive comment. "Where is the man?
Off there alone, struggling to cross the pond? If so,
is he slowly dying, and no human helper near him?"

Returning to the sleighs, Horace stood thoughtfully kicking heel against toe, and peering off
into the waste of the lake at our left. Nothing
was said, yet I knew that he was regarding both
Cynthia and Mary fully as much as he was scan-
ning the ice, though he seemed to be looking past
both of the girls.

"Boys," exclaimed Cynthia, at length, "you will make some effort? You will not sit here and allow a fellow-man to perish without an effort for his rescue?"

" What about two pretty girls, daughters of our neighbors, whom we have invited to go to the singing-school, and who will need rescue if we halt here five minutes more in this death blast?" Horace replied, sternly, resolutely.

"Oh, never mind us," she replied; "we can both creep along down to old Crocker's cottage. One of you—Elisha, for instance—would be willing to lead one of the horses, and we could both of us occupy one of the sleighs."

I did not speak. In fact, I knew too well the futility of any skill of mine in that hurricane. If anybody could do anything it was this man, trained amid northern wildernesses of the winter. The silence seemed long. Horace was still standing, his fur cap now removed, however, and his handsome forehead bared to the wind, as if to cool its fever.

At length he said slowly, answering Cynthia Littlewood: " I will do anything in the world for you. Do you, indeed, wish me to make the hazardous attempt to find Felton?"

There was such a world of meaning in his tone that the girl might—for the honor of human nature she might—have interpreted it. Perhaps she did; but if she did in her heart, she did not in her speech. She was not good enough for the large-hearted fellow, the black-eyed beauty. She turned towards Mary and myself, and asked, in a weak way, "What do you say, Mary Holyoke?"

"It seems a terrible thing to ask any human creature to do," was Mary's response, "yet—" Then she too paused.

We waited in silence again, and we bent to the storm. It was not long, however, but in such times moments seem ages. Looking up in a desperate way, Cynthia cried: "Yes, go if you—"

Horace put up his hand as he dropped his cap upon his head, and gravely insisted on finishing her sentence—"If I love you." Then, with a quick movement, this heroic minister's son and friend of mine lifted Cynthia bodily from his sleigh into ours. I leaped out upon his motion to make way for her, and stood at the head of my horse. In another moment he had haltered his own horse, and handed the strap to Cynthia for leading the animal behind my sleigh. Then he caught his robes out, threw them in front of the girls, sprang back, snatched his lantern from under the seat, shouted "Good-bye, God help you and me," and stole away through the gloom out on to that desolate icy surface.

I never felt before that I was consenting to any man's death, but I did then. I upbraided myself then, and I do now, that I did not protest, craven that I was. But my thoughts were not clear. I was either benumbed or maddened by the unmistakable interest that Mary Holyoke had shown in this lost Felton, this gay teacher of our singing-school. As I plodded on I tried to excuse her, as if her gentle pity was only natural to a woman who thought of a man as perishing, but my wits told me better. There had been more than mere humane feeling in Mary Holyoke's assent and encouragement to Horace Parkridge's heroic endeavor. I felt certain that had she not been jealous of Cynthia Littlewood's interest, if she had not had some springing love for the same man whom Cynthia loved, she would have been as positive as Cynthia in openly urging Horace or myself to go. Was there ever such a mix? And Cynthia recognized that fact in her rival also, for when, twenty minutes later, I got the girls safely into Crocker's warm kitchen, I saw they were jealous of each other, and not disposed to be friendly. In silence we sat together in the warmth of that hut, looking out on that chaotic lake, watching more for the gleam of the lantern than for the breaking of the day.

" Hod hates the singing-master. I just know he does !" sobbed Cynthia, in her half-hysterical excitement, crouching by the window. "I hope they will not get into a quarrel out there in the storm."

I could have boxed her ears ! The idea of a woman who had sent a good fellow to his death, perhaps, and out of love for her he went, taking tearful pity on his rival like that. I rather hoped they would, indeed, have it out there on the ice, all by themselves.

"Boys are so rough!" echoed Mary Holyoke from her window. "Especially our farm boys. But college boys—now, of course, they are more gentlemanly than to fight."

Then I wanted to box her ears more than Cynthia's.

Towards morning the two girls slept a little, sitting in their chairs. I did not, yet I always supposed a woman's heart was more generous than a man's, and would keep her awake in a kind vigil longer. Perhaps I ought to explain it, however, by saying that I was the strongest of the three; or, perhaps, a plain man like me did not read that mystery aright—a woman's heart. It may have been flirtation, not love at all. At length the day broke. The clouds cleared as serenely as if they were meshes of rent cobwebs. The sunlight was brilliant and cold. The landscape was dead. Not a feather's-weight of snow was drifting. I went down at daybreak and saw the sunrise, revealing the further shore of the lake, the factories, the huts of the operatives, the straggling streets, and the church spires, and between them and me the wide waste of uninterrupted wilderness.

There were no tidings for my anxious eyes.

My first duty was, undoubtedly, to return these young ladies to their distressed homes. This I proposed to myself to accomplish by the ox-sleds that broke out the highways. My horse and sleigh would be useless in such drifts. About nine o'clock I got them both safely home to Mr. Holyoke's.

"You, Cynthia, must stay here at Mary's house," I said, as they alighted at the familiar horse-block. "The hired man will go over to your father's with the news of your whereabouts."

"And you?" she asked.

"You must go," Mary Holyoke interrupted promptly, addressing me; "and tell poor dear Mrs. Parkridge and the elder—"

"Tell them what?"

"I see," said Mary; "what can you tell them yet? Now, let me think. I will hang out a cloth in the window towards their house, and they will send over their man, and we two girls will explain what a hero their son has proved to be."

This was decidedly upon the supposition that I would not be there. It greatly relieved me. For I knew I ought to be off.

"His mother will come over herself to learn of her precious boy," remarked Cynthia, uneasily.

Queer girl she; tender heart and cold heart are in one breast.

"If I thought she would," said Mary, "I would try to go over there. Dear heart, she should not expose herself to come here. Or, Elisha, you should go."

"No, give me a cup of coffee and a bit of bacon," I replied, stepping towards the kitchen, "and I must be off to the pond again."

The way I spoke settled it.

The white cloth was hung out in the window at once, according to the country fashion of telegraphing, to accomplish whatever it might effect. I had observed all the morning that the strained relations between the two girls had increased. They did not converse with each other except through me. They both waited on me with eager hands and impatient. They hurried about. They both evidently wished me to be gone on my errand of rescue. But Cynthia made more haste than Mary, quickly coming with plate and cup, though she was in her neighbor's cupboard and pantry. When I rose to go, I said, as I yielded to a sudden impulse, and desperately seized Mary's two hands—I remember well, both hands.

"Cynthia, you are witness. Mary Holyoke and Elisha Stone are engaged to be married!"

It was blunt and farmer-like, I confess; but I had endured enough of agony during the night, and was sure I knew her goodness of heart. I would save her from any infatuation—at least her. The other silly girl might do what she pleased with a passing fancy for a dapper form and bewitching courtier's manner, and repent of it when she must, but this one I would save to her better nature on the spot.

"Oh, are you?" and such a gleam of satisfaction shone in Cynthia's black eyes, as she advanced as quick as a bird ever hopped off a bough and offered to kiss Mary. This I had not yet dared to do myself; and no one was to do it, it seemed, for Mary drew back coldly, repelling us both.

"Engaged, Elisha—Cynthia! Who says so?" objected Mary.

"You will say so," I answered.

Mary averted her face. Cynthia piqued her to assent as adroitly as a fox ever drew a hunter's fire by instantly crying:

"Well, well,.Mary Holyoke, I always said I knew better. The neighborhood said it would turn out so; but I always said I was wiser, and you wouldn't have any farmer boy."

"You were very wise, Cynthia Littlewood," she replied, in haughty scorn. For a moment she almost ceased to struggle with my hands, as if Cynthia's thrust had carried its point.

"But not wise enough to know your intentions? Humph! You will not say him yes, now," said the black-eyed minx.

"Miss Littlewood!" exclaimed Mary Holyoke.

It would have felled me to the floor to have suffered under that look of Mary Holyoke's eyes, and that tone of her kindly voice. Cynthia laughed, however. She had the most musical laugh of any mortal, but in this case it was as cold as the sunlight that fell about us out-of-doors. She was losing her skill rapidly, for she immediately added:

"No, tell him, for he is as noble as—as Horace Parkridge—yes, tell him what I have not yet told

Horace Parkridge, but what you ought to tell Elisha Stone — that you and I are, like two simpletons, in love with Arthur Alfred Felton."

"Cynthia, Cynthia, are you crazy?" The blood
mounted to Mary Holyoke's cheeks as if she had
been listening to some vulgar word or insult, and
the one hand that I still retained struggled to free
itself to fly with the other, which was putting back
the straggling locks from her scarlet brow. Perhaps I misinterpreted her. I have thought it over
many, many hours since then. I should have understood that this mantling color was the shock
to her maidenly modesty. And yet, I do not
know. Perhaps after all those patient years I
have lost my own patience. But the grain had
seemed so ripe for the cutting only fifteen hours
before, when we sang the hymn in the school. A
thousand, thousand times since then I have been
over and over that scene there in the kitchen, and
pictured it that, at Cynthia's words, Mary gave
me both her dear hands, and looked up into my
eyes with her own sweet lips speaking some reassuring vows, as steadfast as the eternal hills, and
so sheltering herself against the indelicacy of her
fiery friend's open declaration of an improper
thing. I have pictured it over and over that I
kissed her lips then and there, that had uttered
the vow of my reassurance and my happiness.

But, no; it was far from that. I replied indig-
nantly to the Littlewood girl, and looked only at
her:

"You simpletons," I said, "the man is dead! His black curls are under the ice."

"Never, prophet of evil!" Cynthia exclaimed, her voice even shrill, though it was too sweet ever to be shrill, as she flung herself away to look out of the window, thinking some fresh news might have come.

Mary, as befitted her more gentle self, said: "Oh, God forbid!" and turned towards the door.

I stepped with a heavy foot in front of her, opened the door, and left her standing there as I went out. I was no wooer; I ought never to have gone without her kiss. I was a fool. I strode along past the wood-pile, where the sawyers were at work behind the horse-power, and shouted:

"Come on, boys, I want you all down on the lake. We have lost the best boy in town, Horace Parkridge, who has perished in the storm."

A sharp and distressful woman's cry came from the other side of the straggling wood-pile. It made my heart stop. I turned. There was the dear little gray-haired woman, Mrs. Parkridge herself, standing in the path. Her huge, raw-boned, ungainly, honest-hearted husband, the elder, was struggling on behind her. Lifting up her hands, her blue eyes searching my face, she exclaimed, "My precious boy!"

It shot me through and through. The dear, glorious soul! we all loved her gentle ways. We knew, the whole country-side knew it, the world of sorrow through which she had so patiently lived by her calm Christian faith. Not a home among us all, where sorrow had fallen, that she had not drawn nigh, and said, "My dears, I know all about it!" and pointed us to her God. All her children, except this one boy slept on the hillside yonder, where the white wall of marble headstones would now have been plainly visible but for the landscape in its sheet of snow.

"Horace, my darling! Oh, why—where—" These were some of the other words that she gasped out, her beautiful brow knit with anxiety, her wavy gray hair fluttering in the breeze, her two hands clasped pleadingly. As if it were necessary by any prayer of hers to wring from me any word that I could bring to her!

"God bless you, dear soul!" I said ; "I am sure Horace is safe." May Heaven forgive me if I told what I did not believe. "He went out to search for Cynthia Littlewood's beau."

A glance of instant intelligence flashed across her features. It relieved her anxiety apparently in a moment. Her hands fell at her sides. She turned a moment to bestow a look upon her husband, who was altogether dependent upon her wits for every guidance when in her company, and then back to me, as she exclaimed:

"I trust to God that my boy finds Cynthia Littlewood's beau!" It was an inexpressible fervor that accompanied these words, and a sigh of relief at the end. There was a double meaning in the words, of course.

"And you do not fear for your son?" I exclaimed.

"Most I fear for him if he does not find the music-teacher alive," she replied. Then she begged for the narrative. She listened quietly to the end, and then said, "Elisha Stone, good neighbor, is she in the house?"

"Yes," I answered; "both of them are in there."

"Elisha, God only knows the purpose of a human life when once he has given it upon this earth, and its limits. If this Mr. Felton is indeed alive, and recovered by my dear brave boy, though it means a momentary pang to dear Horace in his folly, it eventually means his salvation, for she will choose the teacher. Please Heaven, it is so — oh, please Heaven! But if young Felton has perished, then begins such a melancholy life of misery for my son. The boy is infatuated with her. You know how hearty and strong he is in all his purposes. He will storm her heart, such as she has. He will marry Cynthia Littlewood. Oh, father, let us go home"— turning to her husband—"and pray to God to spare the young student music-teacher's life. I could pray for any man's life for his own sake; but for this one—oh, God spare!"

It took me all aback. I had been half hoping— dare I confess it here on this confidential page?— that Felton was under the ice, and for my own reasons. But this woman's ken read the possible future in a different way. I stood silent, trying to take it in. Then, just as I saw she was about to retrace her steps with her silent husband, I said,

"Mrs. Parkridge, the devil has been whispering to me quite a different—"

"Yes, my son, yes, I know"—she called us all in the parish her sons and daughters—"but the Lord speaks a different whisper. If you will excuse me, not only may this young man be alive for his own sake, for I fear he is not prepared to die, but for all our sakes, and especially for Horace Parkridge's sake."

I can see it all, her meaning of wise foresight, at this distance of time, but not then. I turned away, leading my troop of volunteers for the search over the ice, a weary tramp through the drifts down to the distant lake. All these fellows were kind-hearted men, and they chatted as we walked.

"This'll kinder spoil your apple-parin' nex' Thursday, Stone," said Tom Calkins, the boss sawyer, whom I knew well.

"Oh, man," I growled, "it upsets everything for the winter."

"How's that?" asked Jim Peabody, our champion wrestler. "I wanted a chance with that Dartmouth College feller. They say he's science in the gymnasium. I say, Stone, what in tunket is a gymnasium, anyhow?"

I smiled in spite of myself, I remember, at this ignorance of common things in this son of one of our well-to-do farmers.

"I have no heart to talk, boys," I replied.

"Fiddlesticks! Those two chaps ain't dead. You'll hev your big time jest the same, neighbor. All the north district is coming."

CHAPTER III

"HERE's a crowd off on the Weatherboro Cove!" shouted Sawyer, after we had trudged on for more than an hour.

"Yes; and they've found the bodies," I cried, springing forward, for I could distinguish by the grouping of the distant men that they were centred about a particular spot upon the ice. With a wild rush we sped over the intervening distance to the spot where a knot of men and boys were gathered, and towards which other searchers were streaming in from different sections of the lake.

"Hollo, neighbor Stone!" shouted Smith Green, one of our prominent farmers, "I am glad to see that one of your party has an axe. Chop right down here. Come here! See, that is a human head bobbed up on the under side of this 'ere ice. Th' ice is clear as glass here, and mighty thin too. Them pines standin' round here to the southwest allus makes this as gloomy as a grave-yard. I never like to row up here, or skate up here, or come up here, and how in creation a feller could have wandered up here thinkin' he was goin' to West Village is more'n I c'n under-

stand. Them springs of water allus make it poor
freezin' up here. That's my 'xperiunce. There's
another head of hair, sure's I'm Smith Green!
God help us, men, we've found both on 'em!
Gloomy old corner of the pond this, anyway."

While my axe was falling blow upon blow the
tin horns of various parties of search were calling
the signal well known among us in case of a lost
cow or a lost child, telling that the search was
over. My honest neighbors were more or less enjoying the luxury of horrible news, each new-
comer being informed with a shout:

"We've got 'em! Both drowned."

"Hod Parkridge is dead!"

"The singin'-teacher's drowned!"

It was hollooed by boys. It was bawled by
men. It was screamed by some of the factory-
women who had come out over the ice.

"Stand back there!" I cried, as my blows began
to show the leakage of water, and that I was
nearly through. A man reached me a boat-hook
as I had fairly broken through the ice, when just
at that moment, strong as a bugle note on the
frosty air, a voice sounded from the pines above
us:

"Ship ahoy! What are you fishing for? Our
two buffalo overcoats?"

We all looked up aghast towards that south
wall of green, where the palisade of pine and
hemlock was so dense that no pedestrian could be
discovered walking underneath. At that mo-

ment another voice pealed forth, more musical,
but not more penetrating, singing:

> "'Twas off the blue Canary Isles,
>   A glorious summer's day;
> I sat upon the quarter-deck,
>   And whiffed my cares away."

"Gee whittaker!" cried a school-boy, "that's
the singin'-teacher."

"I vum, the first voice was dear old Hod, or
his ghost!" cried a neighbor.

"Hurrah! hurrah!" rang upon the air, as we
realized that in all probability they were no
ghosts, but the men alive.

"Hush! hear the fellow sing the rest of that
song, won't you?" said some one, for we had
drowned out his notes with our joyous exclama-
tions. But now the crowd hushed itself in quick
revulsion of feeling to hear the remainder of his
refrain.

> "It was my last cigar—it was my last cigar;
> I breathed a sigh to think, in sooth,
> It was my last cigar."

Such was the charm of his rich voice—such the
witchery of the devil-may-care spirit in the man—
that still the men waited while the singer, or his
ghost, began again:

> "I leaned against the quarter-rail,
>   And looked down in the sea,
> E'en there the purple wreath of smoke
>   Was curling gracefully;

"But what had I at such a time
    To do with wasting care ?
Alas ! the trembling tear replied,
    It was my last cigar."

As soon as the echo had died away, and the smiles had begun to appear upon the countenances of the men about me, I cried : "Holloo !" And the voice came back :

"Holloo ! 'Lish, old boy, we are all right," and the next moment the two men emerged from the edge of the forest.

It is always impossible not to rejoice with life rescued. I sprang forward to grasp my friend's open hand. The crowd stood around worshipfully ogling the two men, who had evidently come back from heroic struggle, if not from the other world. In his frank and open way Horace began to explain, using the most matter-of-fact language, certainly no boasting.

"You see, I got here just in time, 'Lish. The fellow had broken through the ice. There was nothing for it but for me to go in after him. We both had to strip to some extent, which accounts for our two overcoats, which you thought stood for ourselves, and which I hope you will now go ahead and fish out, for mine cost me forty dollars."

"Yes," said Felton, in a superior, airy way, "the best of all was that my friend and rescuer here knew the farmer on the bank, who took us in, gave us some good dry clothing, fed us, and here we are, all right. How are the ladies ?"

For the first time a cloud fell over the frank and laughing face of my friend. Up to that moment he had been glowing with the consciousness of a good deed well done, and getting his physical equipoise from a night of great exertion. Probably not the slightest mention of what must have been uppermost in each man's consciousness the moment he had come back to the world he lived in had been made till Felton asked, "How are the ladies?" Turning to me, Horace said, in a low tone, which had a sound of severity in it,

"Get rid of the crowd, Stone; I want you alone to hear what I have to say to Felton, and I am going to say it too."

The quick ear of the other man caught the remark, and he was ready. He volunteered, indeed, to relieve us of the crowd.

"My friends," he said, with a wave of his hand, "I am very much obliged for the interest you have taken in me. Next spring I intend to wind up one of my singing-schools, probably here in West Village, with a free concert. Remember, you are all invited. You will get your tickets in season. Now, good-bye; I must look after my horse and sleigh—what is left of them—and the ladies," with a quick, bold glance towards Parkridge, which was evidently intended to be either defiant or exasperating, as Parkridge pleased.

We three started off without more ado by ourselves towards the north shore. The crowd yelled, "Three cheers for Horace Parkridge!"

and attempted a fainter one or two for the music-teacher. Whether the significance of the contrasted cheers was lost upon Arthur Alfred Felton I do not know. I do not think it was needed, this evidence of his strength upon the hill-sides, to nerve the spirit of my friend for what he was about to undertake. We walked on some time in a silence that was almost sullen. I did not even inquire into the particulars of his night's adventure, or congratulate either him or the singer, as I strode along at Parkridge's side. We walked until we must have been mere specks on the blue sunlit surface to all spectator's eyes.

"Now, see here," said Horace, suddenly, "stop! We are alone: God only above us."

"Oh, don't be so pious about it," laughed Felton.

I can hear it now, the light and bantering laugh of the handsome man. "We'll forgive you, however, being a preacher's boy," he resumed. "I say, Stone, you haven't a flask, I suppose, about you? You are all such temperance folks up here in Vermont. If you could only give me some idea where my sleigh is. I say," with a too familiar slap upon Horace's shoulder; "I say, shipmate, there is a splice for the main brace in my bag under the seat of my sleigh, if we could only find it in these drifts along the shore."

Parkridge endured the banter patiently enough, but silently growing more maddened every mo-

4

ment as I could see, I knew him so well. Suddenly he blurted out again :

"No; this is the time." And he turned square around to confront the other, who was as tall and as muscular as himself. The difference was only in the bronze of the farmer and the pallor of the student. Two finer-formed men I never saw square off against each other. Looking Felton straight in the eye, Horace began :

"My boy, I know the world. I have seen as much of the world as you, though now I am, indeed, a plain farmer, for my mother's sake."

"Oh, come on.; what have you to say?" replied Felton. "Remember that you have a friend here with you, and that I am alone."

"My friend is as indignant as I am, though made up on a different pattern, and he is not likely to say all that is in his mind, whereas I am just fool enough to blurt out everything that is in my heart."

"Well, speak it," said Felton, standing back and filling his chest, his fine-cut lip curling defiantly. "Remember that you are two to one—"

"And shall take no advantage of that fact, except to compel you to hear us," replied Horace. "You thanked me last night for saving your life."

"Well, what more do you want?"

"Take that back!" cried Horace, and his right arm bent itself as his great hand forced itself into a fist.

"No, Horace," I exclaimed, instantly springing

to his side, "he is not to be handled here. It is only that he is to be compelled to listen."

"You are right, neighbor," said Horace, promptly recovering his self-possession, "I will forgive the insult. Mr. Felton, I did not inform you last night that it was probably the interest taken by two young ladies in your safety that inspired the necessary courage for my search. It is right that you should know this, lest I take more credit to myself than I deserve, and it is also possibly my right here, and now, to add that I do not fancy your merely amusing yourself at the expense of us simple country-folk."

"Man, what are you driving at?" demanded Felton.

"You know, and Stone and I know," replied Horace, "rural manners are free, and may the best man win. But, Felton, Stone here wants a wife. I want a wife. It is none of my business—it is none of Stone's, I presume—whether you want a wife or not; but assuming that you do, *you don't want two!*"

Horace stepped nearer as he defiantly shot those last four words into the singer's teeth, and his clinched hands were ready at his side as he spoke them.

For a moment the two roses on the singer's cheeks faded out. But the black eyes shot fire; the next instant, and the wild-cat nature in him triumphed. Cunning and calm, he laughed and coughed out: ·

"I guess you two boys mean business. Come on, I want to find my wreck," and with that he showed us his back. His movement was so cool that for a moment nothing was said as Hod and I stood staring at each other. It was only for a moment.

"Then, Felton, we part so, do we?" Horace flung it after him, neither of us having stirred from our tracks to follow, and Horace only turning his head upon his squared shoulders as he spoke.

"Oh, but," the singer tossed back over his right shoulder, as he flirted the long black curls on that side of his face and turned it towards us, "I will be good. I want no trouble with you. I will meet you at Stone's great apple-paring; I shall not return to college this week."

Horace's eyes sought mine with a keen questioning gaze.

"True, I invited him," was my simple reply.

"Our quarrel is on now, I am certain," said Horace.

"Ours!" I asked.

"Well, he dislikes Elisha Stone, and he hates Horace Parkridge."

"Are you quite sure that is the way it lies?"

"Yes, I think so," he replied, as we strode on by ourselves towards the northwest. We watched the solitary form of the singer, a mere moving speck now to the northeast.

"Horace," I remarked, "he will continue his

play with the girls. He probably does it in every one of his schools. It is his manners, his dress, his voice, the fact that he is from Dartmouth and is going to be a lawyer, that charms them."

"While we are milkers of cows and sheep-raisers," said Horace, somewhat bitterly.

"Tut, tut, my neighbor," I said, reprovingly, reading his thought. "Mind your mother, boy; that is your duty. Stick to the old farm, and take care of that dear old pair. Then, too, twenty years from now, if we keep to sober industry, we will be better off than this singer. He is too smart."

"Yes, he has no principle," said Horace, meditatively. "He is going to flash and glitter his way through this big, dark world."

"Right, my lad," I answered. "And do you know what else takes with the girls? I was trying to find the secret of his charm a moment ago."

"No."

"Well, I don't know as I can give it a plain name in a single word," I responded, trying to pick out my expressions with care; "but I can tell you what will rob him of it, and it is in your line, and fair play, too."

Horace stopped me short with a hand upon my shoulder. He seemed to fairly snatch at my yet unspoken explanation. I saw the eager look of distress grow on him by the instant, as I was trying to fashion my sentences before I spoke. I did not dare to be careless, for I knew well the

hot blood in my friend's generous heart. I did not
wish to set him on to assault, Heaven knows. As
I saw his bronzed features turn deeper hued in
his passion of suffering, I began to realize how
much he loved the pretty jade up on the hill-side
yonder. His trouble made him resemble his
blessed mother; just as I had seen her a few
hours ago, when her boy's love affair was flinging its shadows in her face. Putting my arm on
his shoulder, I said:

"Hod, could you throw him at wrestling?"

"What!" he exploded. The thought had never occurred to him.

"Dare you stump him, up at my apple-paring?
You know, we always have a champion wrestling
match on such occasions, when the snow is right—
so that no one will be hurt."

"I see," replied Horace, withdrawing his arm
from my shoulder and plunging his hands in his
pockets—"I see," and he began to walk on as the
thought got hold of him and moved him.

"Throw him, and kill him!"

"Yes, throw him if I can. That, you mean,
would kill him with the girls, who are fascinated
by his fine appearance?"

"Well, Hod, you know our country girls as
well as I do. You know the old stories of the
histories and poets, the tournaments with brave
knights and fair ladies. It is the same thing."

Horace began to smile, and pushed his hands
still deeper into his pockets.

"And you think that this romance of chivalry survives still to some extent up here among the Vermont hills?"

"*Think*, boy; I *know* it! I tell you, this at least is true. You just throw that fellow with the hip-lock, in sight of all our young people from four districts, in the snow of our front yard, and you have killed him. After that he is nothing but a singing-schoolmarm, with pretty manners."

"'Lish Stone, I will try it; but are you sure I can do it? Never mind, I will try it. If I fail, you, who are by far the stronger man—"

"No, no, I am a plain log-lifter. I could kill him mowing or chopping logwood, but he is trained in gymnastics, and nearly as athletic as I am, anyway. You have been a sailor, and have had some experience; besides, you have got more wind."

"I will try," Horace said, meditatively.

Nothing more of interest occurred in that conversation, for we soon parted at the forks of the road, and Horace went up towards his father's. I went back to give the good news at Mr. Holyoke's that the lost were found.

CHAPTER IV

"Tu' sheruff's up here yisterday nosin' 'roun'. I s'pose yer house-keeper's told yer?" It was my hired man, Peleg Rumney, who said it, as we were pulling out the coarse remnants from the sheep racks.

It was Thursday morning, the day of my big apple-paring.

"The sheriff!" I exclaimed, and turned around on him with amazement. Nothing so alarms a countryman as a visit from that functionary of law. Jack of all trades, he does every kind of work, from serving writs to detective investigations.

"Eup," responded the little hunchbacked Peleg—which vocal sound was his way of saying yes—bending again to his fork, "driv up with Deacon Littlewood the day you was drawin' oats to th' village. Deacon Littlewood was roostin' on th' top rail o' the bars, talkin' with me, while the sheruff went inter th' house."

"Deacon Littlewood, too, that sanctimonious—"

"Cuss, eh?" chuckled Peleg, lifting his fork-ful. Peleg shared the common prejudice of all sinners and some saints towards the smiling,

black-eyed, shrewd deacon. I caught myself, I
think I may safely put it on record here that I
caught myself. I did not say the word that
Peleg did, for though I was not a member of the
Church, and had only been what our folks call
thoughtful the preceding winter in the school-
house meetings, still I never forgot the fact that
Mary was a member of the Church.

"Peleg," I demanded, as soon as he had cast
his forkful down, "what did the sheriff say to
you?"

"Wa'al, Mr. Stone," he said, plunging the
tines of his fork into the earth, and leaning his
arms on the end of the handle, "uv course yer'll
ask th' house-keeper 'bout his wantin' ter know 'f
when old Bus'orth died, him ez owned the place
before yer did, thet night ther' was a chist up'n
the attic, which she got out fur th' dyin' man, an'
ef she'd know th' chist ef she see it agin', so thet
she'd swar to't."

I hope I didn't turn pale. I had no good reason to, except it might be the second reason that
Peleg himself surmised. God witness that this
farm was mine.

"Don't git scairt, Mr. Stone," Peleg went on.
"P'raps it's coz yer mad thet ye turn so white.
I don't blame yer, speshully ef yer'd heard whut
thet 'ere pious deac'n was cacklin' on th' top rail
o' th' bars, yer know, while he's waitin' fur th'
sheruff ter cum aout."

"I'm not scared, Peleg," I answered, assuming

an case that I did not feel. "Well, what did the saintly man have to say, anyway ?"

"He sed," went on Peleg, leaning still more deliberately across the top of the fork handle, and assuming an important air—"he sed, gazin' 'roun', 'This is a fine old mansion, Peleg,' sez he. An' sez I, 'It's finer'n 'twas when Sen'tor Bus'orth was alive; better kep' up 'n th' fields 'n' 'roun'.' 'Yis,' sez he, 'great, noble house; no wonder it's haunted, considerin' how wicked th' ol' man lived.' An' sez I, 'How was Sen'tor Bus'orth wicked ?' Sez he, 'He was a man of this 'ere present world, lovin' gain more'n godliness, servin' Satan,' sez he." Then Peleg paused.

"What about my house being haunted ?"

"Mr. Stone," replied Peleg, pulling the fork out of the earth and putting it in a new place, "did old Bus'orth have a wife ?"

"Yes; and she was driven out and died in the almshouse, so they say. I know nothing about it."

"'Zac'ly, I vum! An' a darter ?"

"No; there was no child, so far as I know. My deed was signed by the Senator's brother, who is a doctor living in Nashua, New Hampshire." I explained this to Peleg more because I was thinking out loud than because I cared to say anything of my affairs to my hired man.

"I vum ter Moses! I know'd yer was sound. But the singin'-teacher's a lawyer, ain't he?"

I took the old man's breath away as I exclaimed, "What has the singing-teacher to do with all this?"

"'Zac'ly, I vum!' said Peleg, waving his hand over the top of the fork.

I then remembered myself, and concluded that it was not worth while to think out loud in the presence of this old servant. So I turned to him, and laid it down coolly. "Boy"—though his hair was white I always called him boy—"this ghost story : don't you ever let me hear a word of that sort of talk from you again, or you can't stay on this place."

"I know'd it!—I know'd it!—'tain't so ; an' yit, Mr. Stone, you'd better keep me here 'n ter let me go. Don't yer remember thet night when we fastened up thet door, arter all the furnitoor was moved in the other parts of th' house, 'n' ye'd gone down to sit a while in yer room thet night? Ye was sure a little later th' hosses was loose 'n th' stable, and comin' up 'n my room 'n th' ell ter wake me; an' how 'n th' hall, even on your fine carpet thet ye bought 'n Boston we heerd a footstep b'hin' us—"

"Peleg!" I cried, grasping him, "you old Californian miner, are you also a coward? Shut your mouth! You never heard it again, did you? And you have slept there four years." All the decency there was in me rose up to scorn such stuff and my momentary long-past weakness.

"No, no; don't shake an ol' feller's shoulders

so." He winced, pulling away from my hand that had fallen on him.

"Well, you didn't—now give me the truth—you didn't by any confessions of your own make my dwelling a horror to the town by telling anything of this old foolery to old Littlewood, did you?"

"No, no, I didn't. I love ye, Mr. Stone, an' wanter live 'n' die on yer place. Ye've ben kind to me. I hope ter goodness thet ye'll succeed in persuadin' th' hansum Mary Holyoke ter cum over here an' be mistress; an' ef thet purty gal gits in here oncet, all yer trubbles 'll be over."

I would ordinarily have resented his too familiar reference but that I was bent on controlling the little jackanapes. I believed I could trust the old man, for surely I had been a friend to him, and meant to keep him there until I buried him. So I said no more, but strode around to the front of my dwelling, taking the longer walk to cool off, thinking I would seek out my house-keeper. As I stepped up on to the front piazza, how peaceful the mountains towards the west shone in the splendid stretch of winter sunlight that day! Thirty miles away, how grand the view, how noble the house! I loved the old place better than I had ever loved it. Opening the door, I entered the broad hall that ran from the front to the back of the dwelling. My house-keeper, Mrs. Polly Cark, met me. She pointed to the other end of the hall where, against the round window

that revealed the mountains on the north, stood
dear little Mrs. Parkridge, who had come over
early to see if she could be of any motherly as-
sistance in preparing for my great occasion in a
bachelor's house.

"It's time for you to get your Sunday clothes
on, Mr. Stone," said my house-keeper.

"Mrs. Cark," I exclaimed, abruptly, "there is
a plot against me. Come into my library."

Promptly she answered, putting up her two
hands, "I told Mr. Sheriff I knew nothing about
any daughter of old Senator Bosworth."

"Woman," I continued, intensely, though lowering my voice so that Mrs. Parkridge could not
overhear, "that singing-master has got hold of
the old dark tale."

"What is that to you?" she asked. By this
time we were in the library.

"This," I replied, as I shut the door: "he will
put the deacon up to getting hold of this place—
you know, and God knows, how unjustly."

There never was a brighter woman than Mrs.
Polly Cark. She deceived me perfectly. Without asking my explanation of what could be the
motive of the deacon and the method, her next
apparently frank question to me was:

"Is Cynthia in love with the singer?"

"Yes."

"Is the singer in love with Cynthia?"

"No."

I think now that I can recall the mere flit of a

shadow over her face. But she caught herself, and resumed :

"But he makes the deacon believe he is? I see. He has taken the deacon's measure : property, more property, farm after farm. But Mr. Holyoke will stand behind you, dear Mr. Stone, if you need any money for fighting in the courts. You helped him when his boy took away so much of his money." How sincere a friend she seemed !

"Oh, woman, woman !" I groaned, as I turned away and stood with my back towards her, looking out of the window on the mountains. The facts were the very reverse of any such possibility on Mr. Holyoke's part. I was still on Farmer Holyoke's notes for a considerable amount of money with which he had bridged over his boy's mad failure down in Boston, and even the funeral expenses with which we laid the boy away up here in the snow I paid.

Just then there was a sharp rap at the door, and it opened without waiting for my reply.

"Holloo, 'Lish !" and Horace stood before me.

"My friend !"—I stormed it at him, while he stood aghast to see me, usually calm and cool-headed, so excited—"my friend, that singer has been busy for a week around here. He has been stopping over to Littlewood's. He means to ruin me."

"You?" cried Horace.

"Yes, my boy. Why is it that your mother does not want you to marry Cynthia Littlewood?

What does your mother know of her? It is something in the past, before our day of remembrance."

Quickly Mrs. Cark turned round upon us, as if to remind us she was present, and yet there was a gleam in her face which showed she was not sorry to hear him if he answered my question. At least I have since believed so, as I have pieced things together. But what she said was:

"Really, Mr. Stone, you must get ready; you must, you must! Your early visitors are already driving up." And with that she left the room closing the door behind her.

"Well," answered Horace, with a sigh that was half a groan, as soon as we were alone, walking slowly and thoughtfully up to the window beside me, leaning his broad shoulder against the opposite casement, "I confess I don't know what to advise. I wish this—I would to Heaven I could tear my heart out, and wash it clean of any remnant of affection that it holds for Cynthia Littlewood, but I cannot. She is coming over with the singer. I waited on mother, of course, as father had gone to a preacher's meeting, and I knew I could not be Cynthia's escort. Besides all that, the fellow has been visiting the deacon all the week. He will come over with a fine turn-out. You see if he don't. He seems to lack no amount of money." And with that, as I made no reply, Horace left me to go into my own room to make myself presentable to my guests. I thought he evaded my question as to his mother and Cynthia. I was provoked, but would not press him.

An hour later everybody was there, or in sight on the hill-side driveway. I had to slip off up stairs, change my clothes, and put away my agitation, and appear as happy as an apple-paring party demanded.

"How radiantly the winter sunset streams into your great hall always!" exclaimed Mary Holyoke, as she entered, with my opening of the door just as I got down to the landing. "See, papa," she cried, as she called the attention of her father to the flood of rosy sunset light that always overwhelmed the house as the sun went down behind the distant Adirondacks.

"A beautiful home this would make, my child," was the old man's kind reply.

"Yes, indeed," echoed her ruddy, bustling mother, coming up behind and overhearing the conversation, putting out her hands to greet me with unmistakable cordiality.

I knew it, of course—I had known it before—but I knew it beyond the possibility of mistake after that, that both of the old pair were on my side.

"Good-evening, Cynthia," cried Mary, merrily, as she stepped along down the hall. I turned. I had not noticed before that Cynthia and Felton had already arrived, and were standing beneath the old portrait of Senator Bosworth on the right-hand side of the hall. The light fell softly, and fully revealing the portrait. I had found the picture in the house when I bought it, stained and old and almost invisible. There being no one to claim it, I had it restored in Boston, and hung in its old place.

"Now, father," exclaimed Mary's mother to her husband in a low, quick sentence, "the resemblance!"

My ear caught the word and the idea. Strange that I had never thought of it before. I turned and looked on the face of the girl and the pictured face of the old man on the wall. It did seem to me that I saw a resemblance between the iron countenance and the dark beauty. I remember that I thought I would try and compare them again some time during the evening. But as Felton led Cynthia away towards the great kitchen even before I had a chance to come up and greet them, I could not get the pictured old face and the young face in flesh together again; and it is singular that this was the last time for many a day that Cynthia Littlewood was ever under that roof.

It was not very long before my great kitchen was full. In pairs the boys and girls and men and women were at my baskets of apples.

"I will run the parer," exclaimed Felton to Cynthia, reaching for the machine, as they seated themselves at a table; "you quarter and core." He had skilfully arranged their positions where Mary Holyoke could be tantalized, if so disposed, by every attention that he bestowed—and he did it

5

lavishly—upon Cynthia. Mary had been inspecting a half-bushel of popped corn which I had ordered Peleg to deposit at her feet. He brought it in just as Felton arranged his position with Cynthia. I saw the change from white to scarlet flash a moment in Mary's face. I came to the rescue and attracted her attention. I said, "Here, Horace, you and Mary go at these apples," and I pulled a basket to her feet. "I have to be everywhere, as I am master of ceremonies."

"And I will string them with you, Mrs. Holyoke," said pretty Lucy Tennant, with her white arms bared and a stringing-needle in her hands, as they joined the group. "We old folks, Mrs. Holyoke, aren't anxious to blacken our hands with either the paring or the quartering knives." And as Horace pulled his chair round that made up the circle.

A little while later, as I was kneeling down before the great fireplace to knock the coals out for popping the corn, I contrasted the hilarious jollity of a country good time with the darkness in my own heart; all the more as the laugh of some gay heart rose up, and cries for "more apples!" "philopena!" and what not, filled the room with merry music.

"Name it!" I heard Felton cry to Hannah Castlereigh—"name my apple-seeds."

"Of course I'll name it Mary Holyoke," answered the plague. I was myself startled at the girl's penetration. Felton flushed, Cynthia paled.

Felton protested a moment, and then as the seeds were laid out carefully on Cynthia's rosy palm he bent over and began to sing in a low tone as he counted :

"One I love, two you love, three I love I say,
  Four I love with all my heart, and five I cast away,
  Six she loves, seven he loves, eight they both love,
  Nine he comes, ten he tarries,
  Eleven he courts, and twelve he marries."

"Twelve it is ! Yes, yes !" cried Hannah Castlereigh, as she seized the shapely hand to make sure of no trick. "There are twelve seeds, Cynthia, twelve. Mr. Felton marries the name."

"Miss Holyoke will exonerate me, I am sure, for any complicity in this conspiracy against her future liberty," said Arthur Felton, in an airy way. He leaned back to bring Mary into the scope of their circle. "This is Miss Castlereigh's nonsense."

It was explained in a way, however, as I could detect, to pique Mary. His tone caressed her while his words seemed to put her aside. As for Cynthia, she showed prompt resentment at the fates, and helped the game Felton was playing on Mary's jealousy by saying:

"No; the fates will have it so. You better go and pay court to your future destiny."

"Not at all, my pretty lady," cried he, gayly. "Come," as he pushed his chair back, "you are tired, let's put aside this business. Let me loop your string over the pole, and then let's dance. It is time, and the violins are tuning up." ·

He caught Cynthia's festoon of apple quarters, holding it out at arm's - length, several yards in all, and flung it over the pole that crossed the ceiling nearest him, and then sprung out into the room, crying :

" First set."

But no one responded. I went on popping the corn. I did not look to Mary. I did not need to study Horace's face. I felt sure he, at least, saw through it all. It was Felton's plan to distress Mary, if she had the slightest fondness for himself, by the most exclusive attention to Cynthia and neglect of herself.

" We haven't earned the right to dance to Farmer Stone's music yet," protested Ezekiel Blood, pulling Lucy Tennant into the chair vacated by Felton, and taking Cynthia's place. This seemed to be the general sentiment, with a dozen baskets of my fruit left. And so, while the forty people, old and young, went on with their tasks, Cynthia and Felton started off into the hall for a stroll through the other rooms of the house, arm in arm ; they only reappeared now and then to snatch at the work, for the next hour bothering others more than they helped. They succeeded in starting considerable gossip about themselves, and a by-play of criticism, which I knew Cynthia gloried in, tossing her shining head.

" Miss Mary," I said at length, " we are going

to clear the room now for the dance. You and
Horace—"

"Yes, yes," she replied, nervously glancing up,
the roses on her cheeks glowing as she spoke,
showing the mental excitement under which she
had been laboring for the evening; "but I am
not ready yet."

"I see," I said; "it is a race between you two
and Marinda Joslyn and Tom Calkins to see who
shall get the last apple out of the last two baskets," and I left them at their contest.

"Neighbor Stone," said Deacon Littlewood,
approaching me, "if you'll excuse me, I think I'll
go hum. Mrs. Littlewood and I will now retire.
I do not 'bject altogether to sich vanities, and yit
I can't stay to the dance. Such worldliness
breaks up the sperit of solemn things, which we
hope fur in the school-house meetin's this winter.
Oh, my dear young man, when will you young
folks think on the latter end?"

"Pardon us if we don't to-night, deacon. After all, we are a meeting-going neighborhood, I
believe. There's no one here, so far as I see,"
looking round and turning him by the shoulder
for the same purpose, "who don't go to one of
the three churches—except it may be our friend
the singer." I fixed my eyes on him to study the
effect of the last words.

"True, alas! for him. He's been stoppin' tew
our h'us. He's powerful smart on psalmody and
—and makin' a dollar." Then the man laughed.

It was such a startling laugh. There was no fun
in it. It was like a clinching argument without
words. When he had no more that he wished to
say, or when he thought he could overwhelm you
with empty sound, Deacon Littlewood always
laughed.

"But, my dear neighbor, this is no wicked ball
—a mere country-home jollification. You surely
do not object to that?"

"No, no," with a wave of those hands that always reminded me of bird-claws, "but you'll excuse me, I have to be so keerful;" and out he
glided, his eyes, so black that they seemed all
iris, twinkling as if he had seen the evil one, to
say nothing of me. This excellent man unified his
sinful tendencies. One evil was sufficient for him
to support, especially such as his inordinate greed.

"There are always two opinions about dancing
among our country folks," playfully remarked the
venerable Abner Holyoke. "It does me good,
I'm sure, once in a while."

It did me good always to see this gracious old
man warm up to the occasion, about the fourth
set of Virginia-reel, his squeaky boots tiptoeing
down the centre of the kitchen floor, starting up
the aged splinters from the yellow paint, his
rather solemn face beaming beneficence as his
kind eyes were turned towards the ceiling. He
held his partner's hand so high on this occasion
that little Lucy Tennant seemed mere airy nothing, all in white, at his side.

"Are we really to have a wrestling match, Elisha?" asked Mary, a little later on, when I thought they had danced enough, and I had begun to set in motion the out-door rounding up of our sports. I was passing her wraps to her for the veranda as she asked the question.

"Yes ; you know that is the rural notion," I replied.

"You don't think it is too commonplace, then ?" she rejoined, looking up into my face. "But, of course, you have to follow the fashion in providing for your guests," and she made ready to accompany me, moving on with the throng.

This question of Mary's put a new face on things. I realized that she had in many respects outgrown some of our district habits, our country ways and manners. I had, however, resolved myself not to be drawn into the athletics, which, no doubt, at that time were far from being as welcome among the fashionable world as in later years, but they were fashionable enough then among our country people.

"Glorious moon !" exclaimed young Tomlinson, a student for the ministry, who had enjoyed the rest of the festivities well enough, but who had stolen away to hide himself among my books while we danced, and yet he had no scruples about witnessing "snap - the - whip," "fox - and - geese," and the wrestling in the snow from the piazza.

There they stand on the trodden snow—the

wrestlers. Did you ever witness that fun? It
stirs a man's boyhood soul the recollection of it.
The young men in a circle, but the fair spectators
on the piazza and under the porch having full
view where the circle is broken up on one side.
Coats and hats are off as the proud giants, robed
in white to the waist, are silvered over by the
cold spectator moon. Their blood is up from the
other games, such as snap-the-whip, goal, etc.,
which has warmed them till the little puffs of hot
breath halo both wrestlers and spectators alike
as they stand expectant.

"Who is it?" asks some of the women, as I
pass out another chair.

"Hush! they are getting their hold," answers
the eager Tennant girl, full of the spirit of the fun.

"It is Horace Parkridge and James Peabody,"
I explain. "James is our champion, you know,
in these parts," and I then stepped down into
the throng near the contestants.

The men screw their great palms on each other's
shoulders, with their thick fingers fastening the
grip like a vise. The alternate grasp is on the
elbow. Scarlet necks throb deeper red above
their white neckbands, collars stripped off that
the heavy breaths may heave the more freely.

"Aye! That is a blow of the foot to knock a
hitching post down," some one exclaims, as Peabody's heavy boot strikes at Horace's right.

"But that leg was rooted like an oak," another
answers, "and didn't budge an inch."

Thud! thud!—I hear the blows, and recognize them as Horace's doughty foot in return. But nothing comes of it. I am apprehensive for the boy; I want him to live out the contest, and be ready for the singer next. I have no ambition to grapple with him myself; and unless Horace shall succeed in this bout, then he will lose his own golden opportunity, and Peabody will wrestle with the singer.

"Hurrah!" some one cries.

"No! no! no!" are the answering shouts. These are partisan cries.

I am walking about. I say under breath to Horace: "Steady, my boy, don't fail," but I get no answer. I cannot endure to see them bend each other like withes, and I walk back all suspense towards the old folks and the girls under the porch. The singer is seated there between Mary Holyoke and Cynthia Littlewood. He accosts me with his ringing voice as I approach:

"The sailor is the smaller man of the two by an inch, I should say, and has a hard road to travel. How will he do it?"

"By my wits!" shouts Horace on the frosty air, half savagely, for he has overheard it.

"Then he will travel cheap enough," rejoins the singer, in a low tone; and I notice that Cynthia laughs, though Mary does not.

"Heigh! Heigh!" I turn. They are in the grapple. We all hold our breath. It seems an age. It is but a minute, and it is over. Down, down—Horace throws the champion !

I am the first to take my friend's hand as he approaches. There is a silvery hurrah from the piazza, a waving of handkerchiefs in the flash of moonbeams. I do not know who is in the cheer from that group yonder, I would give a good deal to know ; it would tell the trend of sympathies.

"Who will take him ? Who will take him ?" cries Peabody, as Horace is offering to put on his coat. "No, no, you are the best man. Who will take him ?" And the vanquished giant grasps him by the shoulder.

"I will take him," answers the fine firm tone of the singer voluntarily, as he stalks along across the snow, casting off his garments as he strides towards us. I, of course, carry his clothes back, and deposit them at the feet of the women.

"Oh, my boy is too weary," protests Horace's mother.

"Yes, indeed," answer the women. Still they have small pity, being at fever heat of excitability. When had fair lady at a race-course ever pity for the colt that carried her wager, or in the coliseum, or in the old days of the tourneys of which Scott has told us ? There are no wagers here, to be sure, but the hopes that are hanging, the pride of friendship, are equally pitiless in their urgency.

Meanwhile the men are linked and playing their stern foils and bluffs.

"What do you think, boy?" asked Father Holyoke, as I am turning in and out nervously, and finally start to go back towards them.

"It is Horace's breath," I answer. "It is only a question of his breath, I think." I attempt to stand where I am. I dare not trust myself to go down towards the athletes. My interest is so intense that I know I could not hold my tongue. I fear that my turn will come next. I must not forfeit the good-will of my guests by showing my secret partisanship, so I fold my arms across my breast, and lean against the trunk of the little cherry on the right of the step. After a while I cry: "Don't spend time in skirmishing, Hod."

I cannot help shouting it. I regret it the moment it has passed my lips, for Cynthia Littlewood reads me as she whispers: "Shame, Mr. Stone! Have you bet on our neighbor?"

"If there are bets—" Mary Holyoke begins to protest.

"No, no, girls; there are no wagers." I toss this over my shoulder, not withdrawing my eyes. "Can't an old school friend wish to see his next-door neighbor hold up the honors of the North District against a stranger?"

My word has helped Horace. They twist at the arms, they hasten to the grapple; they strain each other, as a heavy wind sweeps over the trees when they are full-leaved. I walk down nearer to them, arms still folded, striding on step by step, my eyes seeing nothing but the contestants. I read Horace's face, especially as I notice that it has grown pale. It is that question of the breath of which we spoke. Oh, if he were not a smoker! That comes of his sea life. The back of the neck is bursting with color, the cheeks grow whiter still. His pulls are terrific, and fairly lift the other man, but his foot blows are feebler.

"Horace," I murmur, in a low tone, as I foresee that his nerve is failing, "you cannot do the thing you are thinking about."

But I am too late. Horace tries it, the hip-lock; as he half turns for the throw the singer strikes at his left foot, which is to be the fulcrum. Oh, oh, it slips! He reels — is down! Hurrah, hurrah, the singer is victorious!

"Stone, St—" Horace cries it at me with what breath he can gather, as soon as he is upon his feet. I see how death-like the dear face looks. I feel such a surge of vengeful strength rush along my bony arms! I am ready for the victor, but I wonder at my own boldness.

"Not yet," cries the crowd, taking the part of the victor; "give him breath." But I regard it not, I am so eager; I throw my garments on the back of my friend. This shall be a truthful biography, cost me what it may to always confess my own secret heart.

Horace answers, "The singer has as much rest as I had." But I suddenly bethink me, and I respond, "Still, I will give him time to breathe."

It is difficult for me to resist the impulse of my heart, but I insist upon it.

"Yes; give him rest. I will take a bout with Peabody to equalize myself. Then let me try the champion, Mr. Arthur Alfred Felton." Jim comes to me, and we are at it. I need not recount the narrative of this unimportant contest, as it was only to put me on an equality with the champion. I am surprised by my own strength. I am ashamed to confess it, but I write this story for the truth in all particulars: I assert, and I may as well confess it, that there is a sense of anger in my heart. All the time that I am struggling with Peabody I imagine that I am grappling with the singer. I cannot forget all the plotting on which I have stumbled where he has sought nothing short of my ruin in the last busy week of his cunning life. After a few moments I break Peabody over. Then I cry, "Come on now!" I excitedly stretch out my arms towards Arthur Alfred Felton. "Come on," I say. I am panting like a war-horse.

"He comes, eagerly"—Horace says it to me under his breath. I can to this day feel the swelling muscles of that shoulder and that subtle elbow under my clutch. We look each other in the face just once before we bow to it, and in that stare, all smiling though it be, I see his malice. We are to strive, and we seem to know it, for the very ground beneath our feet. Yes, for home, for place among men, for friendship and

for the loyalty of woman's love. Instantly he
steps upon my toe and pulls me forward. I answer him. I come on him like a log-heap.

"Heavens, man! You are an avalanche!"

"And you are a panther!"

It is gymnast and ploughman. He knows a
score of little tricks that I have never learned.
As I twist at him he breaks his hold. It is un-
fair, but there is no umpire except the public
opinion of the homely neighbors. They, however, cry out, "Oh! oh!" It is a derisive cry,
and against the singer.

"Man," he protests, "your fingers are as coarse
as spikes."

I have no doubt of it, for I feel even now his
flesh where my corn-husking fingers have worked
through his garments to that white shoulder, his skin like satin drawn over iron. But
I must not let him play another foul trick upon
me.

It is lurch and labor, it is tug and strain and
stand fast. It is many a thundering thump of
my cowhided right foot, and return of lightning
stroke from his patent-leather—his left foot is as
well trained as his right. As we work our eager
way in the excitement of the contest nearer and
nearer to the house, I hear Cynthia Littlewood
exclaim:

"Of course he will. He is the finer make of the
two." I know it is a compliment to the singer,
and full of hope for his victory.

"It is too exciting," answers Mary Holyoke. "I wish it were over."

"It will soon be, my dear; but it is just splendid!" rejoins the dark woman in reply.

I remember that I see the Cark woman among the other maids at the corner of the house. Her gray eyes are like fire. I think at first that it is in sympathy with me that her eyes are so kindled. As the years pass on I learn to know better, do I not?

For the second time this man attempts to maim me. He grinds his small, tapering heel on my toe.

"Foul," I growl; and, strung up to my utmost, I turn my right side. I call all within me to the pillared strength of my left limb which he is pinning down, and I take him — oh, the memory of it!—I take him over my right hip. It is an awful twist of main strength. He lifts! He is clear of the ground! I have him! Over, over—thank Heaven, the thud with which he falls to the snow!

"Curse you," he mutters, white with rage, "I will throw you in another way yet!"

I am upon the point of rising, as I ought to do, when he spits his venom at me; but I am indignant and I do not let him go, though I do not reply. I silently grind him into the snow, my right and my left hand upon the shoulder make the complete touch-down—yes, I grind him into the snow!

I can write no more to-night—at least I will not, lest I put on the paper how often since then

I have wondered in my innermost thoughts if it had been for the happiness of us all had I unwittingly killed him by his fall. God witness that until he cursed me I had no thought of harming him.

CHAPTER V

"You manifested unmistakable anger, Elisha Stone," said Mary. It was two weeks later that I was calling at the house of my neighbor. Meanwhile I had been to Nashua to have my interview with old Dr. Bosworth, the brother of the Senator. My lawyer, Ashael Keep, had been with me.

"Mary Holyoke," I replied, " you know something of my provocation. I knew on that day that this mischief-maker in our once happy circle here was intending to attempt my ejection from my dwelling and place among men."

"*Your* home, Elisha Stone?" There was a coldness in her tone that froze me to the bone.

"Yes, before God, it is my home! I put five thousand dollars of my own into that old place. I do not come here to-day to build up the broken dream of all the years since first I knew you, a pretty child, Miss Holyoke. I have not been utterly uninformed of all the events which have taken place since my apple - paring in this neighborhood. Probably all that fond old dream, as I have called it, is over forever. But I do come here to save my own good name and yours."

"Mr. Stone, be careful!" said Mary's mother,

6

excitedly, stamping her foot. "Mary's good name, say you?"

I caught her rolling ball of yarn and passed it back to her; and then standing in this house, uninvited to be seated, where two weeks ago the easiest chair was mine, I continued:

"Yes, Mrs. Holyoke, you shall all hear me. That fellow Felton is the moving spirit of this lawsuit to defend, as he boasts, an orphan girl's rights, forsooth," and I did not quite suppress my sneer.

"You must have known that Cynthia Littlewood was Senator Bosworth's child." There was something killing in the calmness with which Mary Holyoke charged this fatal knowledge upon me.

"God forgive you, how could I know it? I declare to you that I never knew it."

"Well, it is said that you have just been to see her uncle, who fraudulently inherited her property," added Mary.

"I have, indeed, been down to see old Dr. Bosworth. Into his hands I paid the purchase money for the place. My savings-bank book will show that the money went that way, every dollar to him."

"But would it show what he paid you back?" Mrs. Holyoke said this. I could hardly believe my senses that in so short a time this home, which had always been friendly with me, was bristling with so much opposition and cruel doubt of me.

"Madam can you believe that cursed lie?" I cried. "I know this Felton's case. He proposes to prove, does he, that I was in collusion with a man I never met until I offered to buy the place, which I was told he inherited, and which I had always desired to possess. He proposes to prove that this stranger gave me rebates, as they are called, of nearly half the purchase money, upon consideration that I should help him to conceal the fact that Cynthia Littlewood was his brother's; that is, the old Senator's child?" I am a slow talker, and when I am excited I cannot make long sentences. My indignation and my sorrow choked me, and I stood silent.

"Well, we know that the Littlewood's never had any children of their own, and adopted this one," said Mrs. Holyoke.

"That may be," I resumed, "but I never knew it until now. Whether the rest of the young singing lawyer's plot is true, I am equally ignorant. I propose to try proofs with him. He makes the grasping deacon think that he can prove that the night on which poor Mrs. Bosworth was driven from her home—she being a young thing, the old tyrant great man's child-wife—that she left a little baby behind her, that the Senator forcibly detained it."

"Well, it is true, we know"—Mr. Holyoke, for the first time taking a part in the conversation, sadly put in this—"Mrs. Parkridge and the elder also know that Senator Bosworth's wife died in

the almshouse, from the exposure of that night
of her Hagar-like flight. It was in the winter
of—"

"Yes," Mrs. Holyoke interrupted, "the next
night or two the Senator sent her baby after her.
Mrs. Cark obliged him by undertaking the shock-
ing business from first to last. It was the same
night that the old scamp died of delirium tre-
mens, it is reported, which is bad enough, but
Mrs. Parkridge and the elder whispered to me
that it was more likely of mind horrors that the
old wretch died."

"I am obliged to you," I remarked. "Whether
you really wish it or not, you are helping me.
These facts are some of them new to me, and I
do not think that my lawyer knows them either."

"And the Cark woman took the child in a
wooden chest," resumed Mrs. Holyoke; "she left
it at the almshouse, not knowing that its poor
dear young mother was lying stark dead at that
very moment. The Cark woman supposed that
the mother would claim it; but as it was un-
claimed, the matron of the almshouse called it
"the little wood-chest brat." That is how it got
to be called Littlewood. And that is the way it
attracted the deacon's wife's attention. That is
the way, don't you see? Otherwise they never
would have adopted it. And I think the elder
tried his successful tongue at persuading the
selfish pair. He was always trying to empty the
poorhouse. But I don't think to this day that

the deacon and his wife ever heard the explanation of her birth from Elder Parkridge and his
wife."

Mr. Holyoke turned away, the memory of those
old days stirred his heart, and his eyes moistened
with feeling.

"Whether the deacon and his wife knew it at
the time, they know it now, as they think, from
Mr. Felton, and are eager for my acres."

"*Your* acres?" objected Mary, her glorious
eyes looking a world of mournful reproach
upon me.

I turned to her; I had thought that my heart
had surrendered her image, but to be misjudged
like this was terrible. All my love for her was
suddenly re-enforced by my wounded self-respect.
Confronting her as if she were alone in the room
I said :

"Mary, Mary, I can't endure this. If you tell
me that you love this man, and I have little doubt
that he at least wants to marry you, I shall pray
God to give you what happiness you can get yoked
in with him, but I pray the great God above us
to help me that you shall not count me a dis-
honorable man."

"Elisha Stone, I don't think I have given you
any right to speak to me of my possible marriage
with him or any other person."

"Hear me. Whatever you do," I resumed—
"whatever you do, I shall live from this hour
not feeding on any straw of hope of your love in

return, but eating the fat grain of my self-respect, which I am bound you shall regard. I will live to show you that I am an honest man. I could give up the home. It is naught to me if you are never to be its mistress."

"How can you be right, Mary? It can't—it can't be!" The words fell from Abner Holyoke with a sob, as the old man rose up and started towards the door to the kitchen.

"Father," protested his wife, in her alarm going after him in his feebleness, "let's not open our lips again. Ain't our Mary the wisest person in this house? Ain't we given her an eddication of the best?" In her great excitement the little polish she had gained rubbed away, and the vernacular of her girlhood returned.

So the old pair went out, and we were alone. Mary rose to confront me. It seems but yesterday as I look back upon it all now; the sun shining softly in at the farm-house window—that new bay-window which I had myself planned, where the dear child's geraniums and roses outlived the winter; the window that looked across the hills to my own, the window towards which I had turned so often, saying, "She is away at school. Next week, day after to-morrow night, the lamp will be burning longer." I say, she stood there in the rosy beams of the sunshine, so fair, and yet so resolute against me. I forgive her. In her mind I know that I was at that moment a base man. I was a schemer who had won my acres by conniving to the basest fraud of taking them from an orphan's hand.

"Elisha"—her voice trembled—"I do not love Mr. Felton. His gallantry may have pleased me for a passing moment. I was foolish, but I have put that all away. I might have loved him but for one thing."

"What say you?" I asked, eagerly.

"But for this one thing, that he has been the instrument in the hands of Providence of shattering my ideal of a true man. Could a woman ever love an executioner, however just his office, and especially the executioner of one whom she had revered?"

"O God, give me patience! Dear girl, why, his destruction of me is his argument to gain your favor."

She flashed it out at me: "He should marry Cynthia Littlewood."

"Never!" I replied.

"He has as good as asked her hand."

"And will break her heart as soon as he has got me out of the way."

"Poor Elisha," she replied, "I am most pained to hear you so persistent in your deception of the neighborhood and me. Oh, Elisha, why do you not go at once?"

"Go!"

"Yes; if you stay you may be arrested any moment—imprisoned, possibly."

For an instant I could not realize her words.

I had not thought the fellow could do all that. I stood there a great, awkward, shaking mountain above this little woman's pretty head. She put her two hands at length upon mine, which were clinched. She stroked my bony knuckles, and still I did not answer. My head was dizzy. She allowed her right hand to creep up on my shoulder, as a dove might flutter on a stone wall. As I did not speak, her long white fingers caressed my shoulder. "Go!" she resumed. Her upturned eyes showed such tenderness, but it was the tenderness of pity and grief, for she immediately continued: "Go, and begin life elsewhere anew."

I broke from her without reply. My misery and the madness of despair that has made many an honest man dumb, this she had misinterpreted. When my rage at the changeless fate of things drove me forth speechless she still further misinterpreted me.

At the horse-block her father was standing. "Elisha, poor boy," he sighed, "I have known you as an honest lad when, without father or mother, you came to the farm to work. I have been to you like a father all the years since. I still believe in you." I heard the old man, his eyes swimming, his voice trembling; I did not reply. What was the use? Besides, I am not a man of words. I have no fit words with which to write this tale, much less have I words to speak when the heart is full as a barn bursting with hay. "My dear boy, can I not help you?" he asked me.

"You helped me when I was in trouble. I have no money, I can't to-day help you with money, but I will mortgage my farm to help you. I would do anything to help you."

"Does Mary know I am on your notes?" I stammered out.

"No."

"Promise me not to tell her."

"Why?"

"You said you would do anything to help me. Now, promise me you will not tell her this."

"I see, I see," he said, again misinterpreting my mind, "but I believe you thought you had property when you put your name on those notes."

"Swear it to me!"

"I swear it to you."

I did not tell him that I had bought those notes and burned them to save the house over his head. I did it the day before. He would never know it until the first note fell due. It took the last thousand dollars I had in the world—money paid for wool and crops. I did not tell him, I say. I sprang into the saddle and rode away.

CHAPTER VI

FOUR weeks of unbroken sunshine since the great storm had clothed the earth with a snowy crust stiff enough to bear up a horse at full canter. It was the most remarkable crust on record in the sixty years of old 'Kiah Lowrey's weather tables, kept at his little law office in the village.

As the colt felt my spur she bounded. " I wonder how long I am to be free like this," I said to myself, talking to the westering day; "free to go where I will." It was a glorious sense of liberty. My spirits rose with the motion through the brilliant air. Straight out over the fields I took my way. I avoided the highways. I did not care to meet my farmer neighbors, drawing oats and provender to and from the village, with here and there a load of cord-wood, creeping along slowly between the fencing walls. I would not even return home now.

" Let's go to Round Top, Kitty!" I shouted to my animal; "Heaven knows if I will ever go there with you again." This was a favorite point of outlook up the side of one of the Green Mountains. On summer Sabbaths I often rode up there. On winter evenings, after reading in my homespun way some book on astronomy, I would snatch up my little telescope and trot up there to view the stars. And, besides, each vacation that pile of rocks had been an oft-sought resting-point for Mary Holyoke and myself while our horses stood tethered below at the oak. Years ago we had cut our childish names in the bark. The letters were entirely overgrown now, but I knew what the scars meant, folded in out of sight near to the oak's great faithful heart.

"Holloo!" a voice rang out, clear as a bell-call, above the little crashes of my horse's hoofs upon the crust. I did not note it at first, for riding makes the ears throb in the wind. I looked around and could see nothing. Presently I heard the whack, whack, of a wood-chopper's axe.

"Ah, yes, Kitty," I said, "it's Hod Parkridge, in his own woods yonder. He thinks I don't hear, and has fallen to work again. Holloo, Hod! I'll come in!" and I turned into the edge of the maple and beech forest.

"Come to my fire, neighbor, and let's hear the latest," was Hod's salutation, dropping his axe with a sticking blow into one side of the great chip on the log. He threw on his long blue woollen frock, and walked at my saddle-bow three or four rods further till we came to his sugar-hut. There was a fire smoking down to dulness on the cobblestone hearth, where a few months later sap-pans would be steaming. He replenished the fire.

"I will hitch Kitty under the shanty out of the wind and throw on this blanket," I was saying, when the boy sprang up suddenly, crying out,

"Good-afternoon, Cynthia!"

I turned. There sat the girl in the saddle. She had approached from the other side of the knoll about the same time that I did. We had not seen each other. I stepped back into the concealment of the shed.

"Why, good-afternoon, Horace! I have just come from your mother." Her beauty lost nothing by being horsed. This peerless creature and her animal seemed to fill the great aisled solemn woods with a sudden flash of splendor. Her horse was smoking, and nosed her, as much as to say, "Oh, let me stop and breathe!" She stripped off her fur mitten and patted the animal's neck. The sight of her shapely hand knocked Hod over. I saw him almost snatch at the hand; but instead he put his own hand into the deep pocket of his overfrock, as if to keep it respectful. Then, too, immediately the witch smiled on him. She was after something, I felt convinced, she was beaming on him so. My thought was, as I watched them both over the back of my colt, myself unobserved:

"Why don't the singer take her? To such a man this sparkling, brilliant woman must be far more charming than my great-hearted, thoughtful, slow-moving Mary. Mary's face has the beauty of a July noon; this face has the beauty

of a sparkling, dewy May morning." I leaned
on my saddle, and, hidden there, studied her. I
pitied her. She was too beautiful to be made a
cat's-paw for my destruction, and then herself
to be rejected by that scoundrel Felton. In my
compassion for her imagined fate I almost for-
gave her any injury she might have lent herself
to regarding me.

"Why don't you ask me to your fire, Hod?"
she said, freeing the stirrup-foot at the same time.
Then she put down that wonderful hand on his
shoulder. Instantly Horace dropped on one knee,
and gave her small foot a chance to pounce on
the horse-block which he made of the other knee.

"He is her perfect slave," I commune with myself, "and the man who comes between him and
his heart's mistress will suffer. Where will all
this end?"

The pair stepped along the snow to the fire. I
was concealed still, and the love-mad boy had
forgotten, probably, my existence.

"Yes," she remarked, clutching back her riding-habit, and pushing her stout little boot against
the front log till the sparks shot up about her
and made her spring back to save her skirts, "I
have been over to Mother Parkridge's. I love to
go there. She is the best soul in the country-side.
She is good to everybody."

"It has been a long time since you thus favored
us," Horace replied. He stood because she stood.
If she had sat he would have sat down at her side.

"I confess it, Horace, but—" and then she sank on the slab bench in front of the fire. Down he sat also, but at the end of the bench, his hand half bearing his weight and his form bent towards her reverentially. His fine massive face was fairly reverential—I am sure that is the word I want. I recalled that remark of his made in my library —made the evening of the apple-paring, "I wish I could tear my heart out and wash it clean of all love for Cynthia Littlewood, but I cannot." And now I believed him.

"I know my mother made you welcome," the host resumed. "Have you been surprising her and father by staying to dinner?"

"Yes;" and she seemed to me to be hunting for the best way to begin her selfish errand.

"I wish I had been there, Cynthia," blurted out the honest boy. How completely real honest love does prostrate a man! Here was a magnificent fellow, well off in the world, with a great noble heart to give, a loyal friend of mine, and himself persuaded that this handsome girl was plotting my destruction, conscious that he himself had been made the laughing-stock of the town by her at the singing-school and at my apple-paring, by her giving him the mitten and choosing the singer, yet now, with one swoop of the splendid bird down on him, ready to sigh like that—"I wish I had been there, Cynthia!"

"Yes," she answered, demurely. Then suddenly, in a most business-like way, she sparkled it out to him, pursing up her lips : "Have you lost any sheep lately by the wolves ? Father wanted me to ride over and ask you what you young men who owned rifles were going to do about it ?"

Horace's countenance fell. It was a mere matter - of - fact errand like that, was it ? It meant, would the young men of the neighborhood organize a hunt and "clean out those varmints," whether wolf, bear, or dog, which were poaching on our upland barns ?

" Is *that* it ?" exclaimed Horace.

" Yes, and—" But she did not finish. I felt sure that the important part of her errand was hidden behind that silence, but she only cut the snow with her riding-whip in circles a little nearer and nearer to his person every stroke.

" They are possibly catamounts," remarked Horace, in an absent-minded manner, with a tinge of disappointment in his tone. " Every long winter, when snows are as deep as this year, and the cold is severe, we get these wolfish dogs or wild-cats, which creep down southward into the States. They come from Canada and the Adirondacks. It is too bad. Has your father lost many sheep ?"

" Why, night before last our open barn, under the shelter of Round Top, where father has so much hay and keeps one flock—well, four lambs in one night and two ewes."

" This is indeed serious. We will try the rifles to-morrow. I will get Elisha Stone—"

Her dark face turned pale at the mention of
my name. Such a subtle spirit could for a time
mask her purpose and deceive any one, much
more Horace; but she could not control her
mantling blood, and her tongue proved traitor,
for she exclaimed, "*I hate him!*"

"Don't say that, for it hurts me."

Thank him for so much. I wonder that he
had the self-possession in his passion to say even
that for his friend, and his tone trembled as he
said it.

"I wonder that you care now, Hod Parkridge,
whether I hurt you or not. I have treated you
shamefully lately." By this meek confession she
had him again instantly, and she followed up her
advantage. Leaning over towards him in an engaging way, graceful in every movement and fascinating, with great emphasis she finished her real
errand,

"Why doesn't Elisha Stone marry Mary Holyoke and done with it?"

"I wish to Heaven she would have him; but
you know why he does not." The man's voice
had got its sternness all in an instant. The neighborhood trouble stood before him like a full-armed
hobgoblin.

"No; I don't know why," she wheedled, soft as
music. "I am Mary's friend; I hope she is
mine. I have taken this journey upon myself for
the sake of all of us. I have been over to see
your mother. You know it is said that I am

wronged out of some property by Elisha Stone. Papa wishes me to push my claim, but I don't want law, law, law. I am too fond of enjoying life and having a jolly time. I only want to be happy, and I want others to be, and I will give it all up, this fight about property, if only Elisha will go and marry Mary ; otherwise "—and her eyes flashed ; she lifted up her small hand, and it was in the shape of a fist—"otherwise I will send him to prison !"

Alas, for the poor boy ! Why could not Horace have seen through it all? But no ; he was as ready to be blind as she was to blind him. Springing to his feet before her, he said :

"And if I will help this wish of yours, or if I make sail for your friend Mary, and of course my friend too, for everybody likes her far and wide, by trying to bring Elisha to the point of popping the question—"

"Then—why, then, you shall have my everlasting blessing, Hod ! I will love you as the best, the dearest neighbor, the noblest fellow in all the country round."

She put both her hands out towards him and grasped one of his. Then she gave him the full look of her black eyes. But it was either too much or too little, such an assertion of thanks. The dear boy returned her such a truthful look, forgiving all and yet asserting all, that she quailed. He seemed to ask what this meant so

7

honestly that she looked up and then around, and started back alarmed. Releasing her hands, she cried,

"Oh, oh, it is sunset! We are talking too long. I must hasten home. Help me to mount. What if I should meet some of those hungry beasts?" and away she flew to her horse.

She had been careless of the colt, and the graceful beast was trembling with the chill of departing day; but Cynthia was soon in the saddle, with the help of Horace's hand.

"If I had my horse here you should not venture over Round Top alone; and if you will return with me to my barn, I will saddle at once and accompany you home."

"Oh, it is unnecessary. I shall get over into Brookfield lane before the after-glow has faded, no doubt." And so, very abruptly, she cantered away.

Horace stood gazing after her for some minutes. I did not interrupt him. Then he turned to me, and said:

"Elisha, come out. That colt of hers is stiff. I am afraid he will fall. Now, you cannot follow her; she says she hates you, but I must. Through the woods there it is possible there is danger. I lost a calf last night. It is a pack of those Canada dogs. We do not often have them. Now, you go down and get my horse and canter after me, and let me take your own."

"Certainly," I said, stripping Kitty; "but, boy,

do you know who she is probably going to meet over at the Brookfield road?"

"No."

"Well, it is the teacher who is going to her house to supper, and then to his Brookfield singing-school."

He settled himself down in the saddle, his chin dropped, and he was buried in thought. I did not deem it best to help him think his way through all that I had said, though he was evidently reviewing the scene. He was having the struggle over again, doubtless, trying to "tear that heart out." A big heart was that to be torn out. He lost precious time, however. The woods were beginning to turn ashen gray, and blue shadows were deepening on the hills. A winter's night falls quickly. There is almost no twilight. At length, starting up from his reverie, he said :

"I know she is not quite safe. If I meet that other wolf—well, I saved his life once, and I will not let him prevent my saving her life now," and he galloped away to the west.

By the time I had saddled Horace's Princess at his distant stable it was full fallen night. I got away quietly, without disturbing the elder's family, to go after the boy and girl. Only starlight fell feebly over the darkened hills. Still that is a considerable light in our northern world, and I got on fast. From the sugar-camp I struck for the dim masses of Round Top. The rising waves of the rolling land climbed upward from the elder's farm quite rapidly to a moderate height. After some time I stopped and hollooed. The echo was the sole reply.

Did you ever start an echo in the open night and open fields and hear the skirting forests take it up, passing it on and over and under till it dies away? If you never did you never yet felt absolute solitude—yes, felt it, I say. On the third or fourth cry of this "Hod Parkridge, Parkridge, 'arkridge, 'ridge," fading fainter, fainter, and gone, I thought I heard a cry. It did not seem like an honest human cry. I listened until Princess's blowing seemed lighter than a deep breath of wind.

"I say, Hod!" I shouted.

"Hod, 'od, 'od, 'od," ran from hill to hill and rolled faintly along the dark blue valley.

The night was so still in the foothills that I could hear the deep roar from the hemlock forests, on the wind-swept heights over on the Green Mountains, beyond the river. The winds always blow up there. There are townships over there that are solid hemlock. To hunt or fish there is perilous. There is no path. There are precipices hidden away.

"Go on, Princess." But instead the pretty beast sprang to the left, turned her head sharp around to the right, and a tremor ran through her like a shock. Her ears, at least, had detected something that I had not heard. The horse has the keenest instinct for physical danger of any animal except the deer. Both deer and horse seek to escape danger. Horses have poor weapons for a fight.

"What is it, Princess?"—patting her neck—I asked. The same tremor was her reply, then a restless effort to bound away.

"Hark!"

"Bark! bark! 'ark!"

That was no echo. It was a wavering sound as from a moving thing. I strained my ears. I heard it again. Now it was unmistakable, the snapping, snarling whine of a hungry savage beast.

"My God!" I yelled it as if the boy and girl might hear it. My tone trembled with my fear. "It is a pack of them, the Canada wolves!" But there was no human creature in sight to hear my cry of alarm.

Straight on like an arrow we flew. It was that hard winter, and it was those deer preserves in the Adirondacks that had given the savage scamps a lingering home so nigh to civilized folks! Our last town-meeting increased the bounty to twenty-five dollars for every wolf's pelt, but I had never known them quite so venturesome as this before. Why, this was not eight miles from my own dwelling. When I overheard the girl's story at the sugar-camp I smiled to myself at her words. I only thought it possible we were being attacked by stray dogs or an occasional wolf. But here was real danger, for neither Horace nor I was armed. Oh, for my rifle, standing behind the door in my library!

My library! I had forgotten my own troubles for a moment, but the memory of the cosey library, with all my bachelor traps, rifles, fishing-rods, sticks, desk, books, and Mary Holyoke's portrait on the mantel—*my library*, indeed! Should I ever enter it again? The thought made me desperate. Heretofore it had been Horace Parkridge who had done all the brave things in these parts. Why should I not throw away my life and done with it, here, meeting these hungry dogs? They were evidently on my scent. Horace and Cynthia might by this time be clean over the hill and beyond any danger from these red mouths, unless Cynthia's horse had yielded to that chill.

I pulled up on the top of a yet higher knoll in Farmer Hampden's pasture, and dismounted that I might hear the better. The bark of the wolves was now plainly audible, borne on the silent frosty night. The sound angered me. The late moon was lifting her sickly last half above the eastern mountains. By stooping down I got the light right, and, straining my eyes, I saw them—the heavy thick gray bodies—skirting the woods away back there. They had not yet broken into the open. I wished they would; I might then know the numbers of this uncanny pack. There, they now slip down from the maple covers. They come—one, four, six, one more, seven, another laggard down from the woods, eight, yet another gaunt fellow, nine.

"Princess, we'll show them our heels," I cried, and sprang back into the saddle. "Now, then, over the rail-fence, my beauty."

But the mare had lost her spirit or self-command. She struck the top bar and fell. She was up and away before I could get her. Heavens! the fool! She ran down the hill towards the pack. Horses are such fatalists in danger: they will return to a fire after you have led them out, if left at liberty. The poor beast had hurt her knee. She fell in the valley ten rods back, and the wolves pounced on her two minutes later. Perhaps I was equally foolish. I could not endure the sight. Wrenching a rail from the fence, I ran down the hill, and leaped in among the pack. But a fang is the worst thing to fight except with rifle and powder.

I would not dwell on this but that I wish to leave on record a truthful experience, so rare in New England, that many a modern reader will not believe it. In two minutes the horse was ruined. She diverted the pack, however. Half-dog as the creatures were, they seemed, moreover, to shrink away from a man. But their ribs showed under their mangy gray coats. They were starved to desperation.

Oh, sickening sight to see two frothy jaws tear at the pretty flanks of the prostrate filly!

"Out of life, you beast; and you, and you!" I

cried, as I wielded my rail. Yelp and snarl,
whack of blows : it was pandemonium of growls
and thwacks. Crack ! Heaven help me ! My
fence-rail snapped. I felt a strange sensation—a
rending, piercing, tearing of the leg just above
my boot-top. I knew enough of anatomy to fore-
tell what would come. I should faint soon from
the loss of blood. I always carried a sheathed
pruning - knife in the pocket over my hip. I
reached for it, and the sheath slipped off. The
dog's fangs that held it scratched my hand, but
I used the knife once, twice, a third time. And I
used something better than a knife, my human
cry.

"Hod, Hod, help, help, for God's sake !" Will
he hear ? I remember now the echoes, how they
flew. I can see now the alarmed stare of some
of those beasts' eyes as they looked up while the
echo run and resounded. Then, too, they had
somewhat satisfied their hunger. They were not
Siberian wolves. The American creature is less
desperate and more wild. They began to slink
away at the resonance of the echo. The leader
leaped out first, then bounded off. The pack les-
sened, so I thought. Then I heard the crack of
a rifle.

Death by loss of blood is like going to sleep,
so they say. I slept, looking last, with a prayer,
up to the three stars in the belt of the Orion.

CHAPTER VII

"You must lie very quietly, Elisha." These were the first words that I heard on regaining consciousness, and the sweet full lips of Mary Holyoke spoke them.

My head was swimming, and I believed I was recovering from a faint, there on the snow-crust. Mary was a dream.

"Hod," I whispered, starting to rise up on my elbow, "has the Littlewood girl escaped?"

"It is not Horace. He had just gone home for a night's sleep." It was the real flesh-and-blood Mary Holyoke who replied to me. "It is I, Elisha," she continued, bending over me. "You must obey me, and lie down again." She pressed me back again on the pillow. A fragrance as from a summer land seemed to salute me as this quiet woman touched me with her compassion.

I obeyed her; indeed, I fell back, conscious of my faintness. After a little I got my breath to ask, "Did Cynthia escape?" I thought I would thus feel my way back into the living world once more.

"From the wolfish dogs? Yes."

"What do you mean, Mary?"

"But from the elegant-tiger, no."

"Please do not trouble my poor head, sweet neighbor," I protested, putting my hand to my brow.

"Hadn't you better tell him more particularly about things?" said a soft low voice from near the window, which I recognized as Mrs. Parkridge's. She sat near the window, through which the twilight colors fell. As she spoke she gathered up her knitting-work and rose to her feet, more feeble than when I saw her last.

"I must now think of returning home," she continued; "the night is gathering. I will speak to your father, Mary, or to Mrs. Cark. Tell him some things that have happened in these weeks, then beg him to be quiet. He will be better satisfied with a few words, I am sure, from you than from anybody else. Moreover, the doctor thought it wiser to help his returning intelligence." And she left the room, casting a beaming maternal gaze upon me.

Very promptly Mrs. Cark entered. I do not know what spiritual warning prompted me, but she reminded me of a great cat.

"Tell her to go out," I protested. My housekeeper heard it, and without other orders retreated. As soon as her spark-like eyes were gone the lamp seemed to burn brighter, and the room to glow. Cats' eyes hasten the gloaming.

Mary then sat down by the bedside, leaned forward and touched my head, putting back the straggling locks of hair. To think of it ! That she was under my roof again, that was enough. But no, she was in my own room. She was there as an angel to minister to me, and her cool soft strong palm was falling on my forehead again, again, again, ceaselessly. My brows, you know, resemble an acre in a rough pasture, and are as homely ; moreover, now they were swept by storms of pain till she touched them. But I lay there speechless, and daring to dream that my plain features might have some comeliness under the flutter of that hand.

"You have been very ill, Elisha."

"Yes? How long?"

"It is now the sixth of February."

"Two months of oblivion. Impossible," I sighed ; and the pain came back again in my head.

"You were sadly hurt, Elisha," she replied, soothingly—"you were bitten by those dogs, the wolves."

"Who fired the rifle?" I asked.

"Who but your own ever true friend, who loves you dearly, and would die for you?"

"God bless him, Horace Parkridge. He must have had a rifle then at his sugar-camp, and returned to get it."

The tears came to my eyes, I was so weak. Then I added once more : "I suppose Cynthia got safely home ? Horace left her there ?"

"Yes, Horace left her," she replied. Her great

brown eyes had such a pity on my feebleness as she went on :

"Elisha, I think you must know more of what has happened since you have been ill. You have had a long delirium, the result of the virus of those fangs, perhaps ; but you will recover now, we hope, though it will require some time. I want you to ask God's help to bear what I now have to tell you. I have myself—oh, so ceaselessly !—prayed to Him for you ; and dear papa, who loves you like a son, has knelt many a night here by your bedside praying for you."

The tears that swam in her eyes lent them a lustre that I had never seen in them before. Whether it was pity or love, I could not say. I raised my feeble hand to clasp her own. She suffered it, and, pressing my hand hard, returned to her task.

"You must try to be brave. Can you endure what I must now tell you ?"

A sick man is cowardly weak. Half-frightened by her portent, and yet resolved by God's help to be worthy of her ministry, I answered, "What has happened ?"

"Cynthia and Mr. Felton are to be married."

I drew a long breath of relief. "Is that all ? Well, Heaven send Horace a worthier love !"

"May He, indeed !" she breathed it fervently. Then she resumed, "they are to be married in this house."

"Great God ! has the case been to court ?" I

sprang up in bed as I spoke the appeal to Heaven, and glared at the gentle creature till she moved to the door and softly called :

" Papa, will you come in?" And the dear old soul entered, sinking down upon the side of my bed, and trying by many words which I cannot now set down to soothe my excitement.

" The surrogate has decided, for his part, that the will brought forward by Mrs. Cark—"

" Heavens, man ! Cark — my old witch of a house-keeper?" I began to gasp for breath from very weakness, and that pain in my head at the base of the brain returned as if a hot iron were being thrust in there.

" Try to bear up, Elisha," urged Abner Holyoke. " God help him, Christ help him to bear up !—for you must be removed to my farm-house at once."

" You are innocent of all intentional fraud, in our minds," Mary hastened to resume, arguing her way for my reassurance. " Say what they will in this neighborhood—taught by Mr. Littlewood, for his own defending, of course — say what they will, we believe that you are innocent of any intentional wrong." She fanned these words upon me as if each dash of air were her benediction.

" Innocent?" I groaned ; " I shall go mad !"

" The surrogate himself "—earnestly old Abner said it—" and the elder and Mrs. Parkridge went before the grand jury and prayed that no indictment should be brought in, and God's holy spirit defended you. It is enough that you lose your home."

"Oh, merciful God !" I cried, "if there be a God—can there be a God, and this old grasping hypocrite be blessed in his scheming? Can there be a God, and this young scamp, who says that there is no God known to science, be himself the winner in this black fraud against me?" Then that pain returned at the base of the brain. I grew too confused to trust my tongue. I overheard Mary sobbing, and, as I did not speak, saying to her father :

"Papa, papa, I love him ! But see ! his mind is a complete wreck. Will he ever recover? We ought not to have told him. Oh, we could have removed him just as well without."

Her father was on his knees, holding my hands, praying in one breath, speaking soothing words to me in the next, and saying: "Yes, yes; he will recover. Such a giant frame, such temperance, and such a bride to live for! O God, with Thee all things are possible! He will recover ; but, Mary, remember what the doctors said—open air, and a long time."

Now, I recall all this perfectly. Then I thought I slept. From my sleep about midnight I thought I awoke, and found myself walking in the upper hall of my house. I was carrying at arm's-length the huge old portrait of Senator Bosworth, studying it as I strode along. I went on towards the closed room in the wing.

"Come on, Peleg!" I cried to my man.

"I dassent," whispered Peleg. "I vum, I'm afraid."

"Get your axe, you old Californian!" I ordered. "Open that door! Felton is to be married here. We want the whole house illuminated. Come on, Felton; I will show you every room in it." It was a most circumstantial dream.

"Catch hold of him—restrain him!" I heard Felton cry it distinctly. "He has escaped from his chamber—he is in his delirium."

Then, with a powerful grasp, I thought I caught Peleg around the body, and hurled his little, hard, gnarled person against that closed door. It burst open. Instead of cobwebs and old boxes, dust and emptiness, there stood a creature luminous in white. The room was furnished in luxury. Who was this ghastly shape? And yet, while I asked who it was, I seemed to see Mrs. Cark—I said so. "Cark! Cark! I detect you under your disguise. I now understand you have nested in this quarter of my house. Your room connects by the back stairs in the tower."

At the same time the figure made no reply, and it was transparent—the stars shone through it. I saw out of windows the flush of breaking day, and the rich red colors along the east were perfectly visible through the strange form.

CHAPTER VIII

"LET them breathe, Elisha. The sun is getting warm. Ease up on your yoke, there. Brindle, back, sir. Steers don't know how to work, anyway."

This is the next thing that I remember with any degree of clearness. Horace spoke it to me in a kindly way—much as a father would speak to a child. There I stood in the field. It was early May. We were just below Elder Parkridge's farm-house. I was in the act of driving oxen for Horace to plough. Then the dear fellow pointed at me with one lifted arm while with the other he beckoned to two ladies who were sitting under the old elm by the garden gate. Evidently there was something about me to excite surprise that, visible to others, was as startling as my strange sensations of returning intelligence were to my own consciousness.

"Mary, mother, come here!" he cried. "Elisha has broken his melancholy at last!"

Then he flew over to me and stood staring me in the face, saying, "Smile again, old boy. Thank God, to see you smile! I would give a hundred dollars if you would laugh outright."

"Hod," I protested, "what is the matter with you? Let me alone. What does the deacon want yonder? I see him climbing up on the highway wall. There is his carriage halted, with his wife sitting holding the lines. Attend to him, and get rid of him. Mrs. Littlewood will be impatient. Then come, and we will talk. My head is clearing."

It seems that my remark concerning these visitors was the first connected sentence that had fallen from my lips for many weary weeks. It is impossible to attempt a description of that strangest consciousness that perhaps mortals ever have on this footstool — the recovery from syncope, or brain injury.

Oh, that last clear consciousness of that February night! The figures of my delirium, the sufferings of my mind, as I walked through those three months in cloud and mist, struggling to break the darkness that shrouded me! Then, the next I knew, here I stood, myself again, in the bursting of the May morning. A winter's night; a summer's day! I knew not what had passed in that long interim, yet evidently I had eaten and slept, and gone about my daily task under the kind care of my watchful friends.

Horace turned away from me, and ran to meet Mary Holyoke and his mother, who stopped a few moments, like two startled deer, on the other side of the ploughed furrows, and gazed at me with clasped hands. For some reason they came no

8

nearer. I caught the last part of the sentence
that he flung across the furrows to them :
"True, himself again. But don't mortify him ;
don't notice."

" Yis, brethering "—Mr. Littlewood was shouting it out to us as he stood there, just on the top
stone of the highway wall, north of the field—
" I'm afeerd I sh'll tumble daown some o' yer
loose stun wall." The next instant he had done
so, nearly tumbling flat himself too, crying out:
" Barked my heel a little !" and holding up his
foot to rub it.

I remember that it was that small avalanche of
cobble-stones rattling after the springing deacon,
as he jumped down among the brambles and nettles, which awoke my laughter from its long sleep,
and seemed to give my lucid moments a stability
once more—a good hearty laugh.

Then approaching us, holding his neat, broad-
brimmed straw in hand, and mopping his red
brows, Deacon Littlewood began his usual ora-
tory, addressing himself to Elder Parkridge main-
ly, though Abner Holyoke stood by, he having
been working at laying out the garden-beds.

"Brethering, this is jest splendid," Littlewood
sang out at the top of his voice. " Abigail, toss
me my ambrell from under the seat. Brethering,
so much business lately has gin me the headache,
and I must be keerful of the sun, but we must
'member
　　"'There'll be no more sorrow there.'

"I jist druv over this splendid weather to see yer. The hevings is now droppin' blessin's on th' airth by the cart-load. Sich blessin's soak me thru and thru. To be out in sich showers o' blessin's as this May weather brings 's 'nuff ter stir a man's thankful heart."

His all-black eyes twinkled in a snaky way as he went on: "Brethering, look raoun' at th' hills. 'As th' mountaings is raoun' abaout J'rooslem.' When I left hum I thought we's ter hev a blessid thunder-shower. Them clouds," turning his head on his round-shouldered, thick, well-preserved body, and then dropping his sentences with his glance, "but it's all the same to any man who's humble 'n' livin' right. I kin smile at Satan's rage in a reg'lar rippin' tearin' roarin' storm, sich 's 'ud tear the linin' outer Natur's beautiful spring garmints o' praise, when I know I'm doin' my dooty." Then he gave us that cracking laugh of which I have spoken before. By this time he was near enough to Horace to poke the boy with his lisle-thread gloved finger in the side and ask:

"How's he?" with a dark glance and a movement of his chin in the direction of his thumb, indicating me. Horace frowned, but answered politely enough:

"We trust he is improving. Mr. Littlewood, what can we do for you to-day?"

"Very mysterious complaint, neighbor. I'll speak ter him."

"Don't !"

" Why not ? I only done my dooty."

"Mr. Littlewood," said Horace, sternly, "if
you regard your course as duty, that is between
you and your God; but don't risk further injuring
a man whom you and your family have savagely
wronged, however legally. Don't approach him:
that would be further injury."

"Oh, jist as you say, 'xactly. I guess any the
rest on yer'd ha' done the same ef yer darter had
a five-thousand-dollar farm at stake. Bizness is
bizness an' religion's religion. I keep 'em sep'-
rit. That's th' only way 't yer kin keep 'em both
safe. Religion's too sacred a thing to be mixed
up with this ere airth. It gets easy siled 'f a man
ain't keerful of his religion."

For myself, I was yet standing in a dreamy
awakening. I was drinking in the sunlight, the
sweet air, the breath of flowers; and the faces of
my dearest earthly friends were beaming on me
there. I scarcely noticed Littlewood until, hop-
ping nearer, in a moment more he was bending
over the plough-handles in front of me. He
cried out to Horace:

"Let 'em go. I want t' talk t' yer. Yer take
the whip 'n I'll take th' handles. Let our friend
stand aside. Git up there, Brindle." At the same
time he prodded the nigh beast with the closed
umbrella, which he also clutched in the same hand
that was holding the plough. The steers started as
if they were shot. The plough caught an apple-

tree root, and the handles knocked loudly at the old man's ribs.

"Dan - net! Why, we're all roots here, boy. Easy, Brindle." A fluff of May wind caught his umbrella and opened it. The unusual sight of Littlewood's broadly flaring linen duster and this spread umbrella skipping towards the steer drove the little good sense that the creature usually had utterly out of his head. Away he started, pulling his mate with him over the fields, the plough skipping like a doctor's gig.

"Why, dan-net, boy!" yelled Mr. Littlewood; "they're goin' ter thunderin' lightnin' — good Lord!—inter them brambles!"

Horace and I sprang after the cattle. There were three heifers feeding quietly in the next lot to the west. I smile, even now, over my paper as I recall that scene. When those three skittish young milkers, frightened by the yoke-rings' clangor and the wild charge of the steers, went over the wall into the highway, with bleating voices and tails in air like pennants, I laughed aloud and long.

"Thank God, oh, thank Heaven!" cried Horace, stopping in his tracks and gazing at me. "Now look, old friend, and laugh again; it will be your cure. You cannot understand what I mean; but one of these days you will know, when you are told how long men have listened in vain for your laugh, and have not seen even a smile."

I looked as his hand pointed, and I began again

to shake my sides with laughter. The speckled heifers made a dash past the deacon's wife, sitting so demurely in the carriage on the highway, the lines lying idly on her lap, and her knitting-work over her fingers. The horse gave one tremendous sudden shy and bolted.

"Why, dan-net to dannation, Abigail!" yelled Mr. Littlewood, scrambling up towards the wall through the tangle of brambles and nettles. "Abbie, saw his mouth!—saw him! Pull the bit right and left; and light out, my gal, and get him by the head, or you'll go to kingdom come!" At the same time he began to climb the wall. The next moment his exhortation was muffled by the brambles under which the devoted old man lay prone. Mrs. Littlewood was equal to the occasion, however, so far as her duty was concerned, and sawed the bit promptly enough until she had her beast under control.

Horace and the great long-limbed elder both reached Mr. Littlewood about the same time, and began as gently as they could to extract him from the briers. I was simply useless with laughter. There, while I was leaning against the bar-post, as I shook and doubled, a strange sensation of returning life came over me. The whole of the Creator's bright world of living men and women, of fair fields and glorious sun, was perfectly unveiled to me once more. The luxury of it—that never-to-be-forgotten laugh! The night of horrors, the oblivion of life, the melancholy of that blackness fled away, and memory of men and things and events, and courage, hope, and life — yea, existence — coming again with every breath.

"Easy, brethering, easy!" scolded Littlewood to his rescuers. "Them blackberry bushes o' yourn 's mighty caressin'. Don't tear my duster all ter tattereens. You pull 's if I's a tarnation stump in a burnt piece."

The gigantic elder was chewing his tongue for dear life to prevent unfraternal remarks in return. But finally he straightened up his unfortunate parishioner, in about the same way that I have forty times seen him settle a meal bag on the barn floor, with a thump.

"Thank the Lord! Why, elder, I'm all nettles. That was pesky near"—then, scratching his smarting hands, and caressing himself gently— "near to — why, I'm all opedilldock burrs in my hair — near to costing me twenty-five dollars fer repairs on Cynthy's new buggy. Thank th' Lord! Brethering, I'm always more thankful when I save a penny than fer all my other fleetin' bless-in's here below. We must be keerful of our pennies. Horace, you and th' other young folks don't know th' value of those pesky things, dollars. Money's only for this brief sphere of our'n, and therefore we oughter be more keerful on't while we have it."

Our neighbor was going on with this homily as he pulled himself again into shape, and got down to business in his own thoughts. He was feeling his way back as promptly as could be, to cover his chagrin, towards that serious errand that had brought him here among people whom he knew had every reason to dislike him.

"Now, Littlewood, see here," said the elder, picking the burrs off his neighbor's clothing, "you're well escaped out of that misfortune. You ought to be kindly disposed towards all your fellow-creatures. You've got a suit of dispossession on Holyoke's farm also. To be sure, you say your notes ain't all quite paid, but if that boy there hadn't been involved in this mysterious dispensation of Providence, he'd have paid all that Abner owed you, as he did at the bank for him. Now, let Holyoke go easy. You don't want his goods and chattels, and we'll keep him over here in our house, for it's large enough for him and his darter. Don't beggar two neighbors."

"What do I hear?" I demanded, confronting the two men with amazement.

The elder bent on me a pitying gaze, which was brightened somewhat with surprise and hope. Then he began slowly to address me, his kindly eyes studying the effect of every word:

"Elisha, bless God, dear boy, you appear more like bein' clothed and in yer right mind than for many a long sad day. Come here." He leaned one long arm on my shoulder, while he used the other to draw the venerable Abner Holyoke into the trio. We thus confronted Mr. Littlewood.

"This frugal neighbor of our'n," the elder went on, with a nod of his head towards Deacon Littlewood, "has in his clus way foreclosed a mortgage given in lieu of Abner's note. Littlewood is a righteous man, very righteous. He has got a title to Abner's acres."

"But that don't pay me his debt in full," snapped out Littlewood.

"His debts, man!" I exploded. "I—I paid his debts, as far as I knew, and got releases. I burned the notes."

The old creditor rubbed his chin and smiled one of those guileless grimaces of his, which would perhaps have disarmed a stranger. "Yis, but, poor lad, yer checks was wuthless. You meant to be kind—to make a show of it, at least, fer his darter's sake, no doubt; but the doctors' commission sot on yer mental state, and let yer off as bein' of unsound mind in the upper story. The judge seed as how yer farm was my darter's, and there was nothin' yourn. Yer crop money in th' bank I trusteed."

"Yes; but, you most grasping neighbor, how came there any mortgage on Abner Holyoke's homestead?"

"He gin some ter the savin's-bank, and one to me."

"Man," I raged, "I had paid his notes and destroyed them, and cleared his property."

"Yis, yer poor cretur," swinging his lisle-thread finger at me, "but I trusteed your bank account;

in th' int'rest of jestice I done it, and yer checks
war'n't wuth nothin'."

I lifted my hand to smite this old hypocrite.

That instant I felt something give way at the
base of the brain. It was not a pain—no, not that
old sensation of a black cloud shot through with
chain-lightning, which I had so often felt. It was
rather as if the last hillock of a mountain had
been finally lifted from my neck, and I stood
erect. It was an ecstasy! Oh, it was an infinite
relief, a repose, a joy! It was health, not only
coming back again, but established forever. My
laughter had been the first sign of its return.
The poison blood-clot from the wolf's fang—that
rabies, against which my poor giant frame had
struggled so long, and which would have crushed
a feebler man to the earth—was gone!

"Gone, kind Heaven, I thank thee!" I fervently exclaimed, and with my hands to my brow I
sank upon my knees. "I praise Thee, Lord God
Almighty," I fairly sobbed. "It is in answer to
Mary Holyoke's prayers, the prayers of her godly
father. There is a Supreme Ruler—there is, there
is!"

"Elisha, dear Elisha"—with measureless com-
miseration Horace spake it, as he sprang to me
and began lifting me—"this is too much for you.
I could curse that old fellow who has plunged
you back again into your— Come, let's get on
our feet and go up to the house."

"Mary, come over here!" shouted the elder to

the ladies, who were still on the other side of the furrows.

"I will go and explain why we want her, or she might shrink from encountering our friend here," said her father, with a glance towards the deacon. I noticed for the first time how feeble and broken the lovely old man had grown.

"Yes, go," the elder added; "he will obey her in his most wilful moments." Meanwhile Mr. Littlewood was squared off, his hands splayed out on his hips, his shaven visage and blank stare, with the lips apart, turned up to the zenith. In a curious kind of groan which he had, and which indicated surprise, he uttered, "A-w!"

A miserable consciousness of shame, dashed with anger, swept over me. Fully alive once more to all this splendid world, I remember I asked myself, in consideration of their estimate of my action, "Is this then the pitiable plight of dependence in which I have been living before my kind neighbors of late?" I thought of King Lear in Mary's favorite play. Not that I was ever kingly; though every man is a king, Heaven knows, who has his senses, and an honest man's place among his fellow-men.

"Don't you dare to pity me, Deacon Littlewood!" I exclaimed, bounding to my feet. "Hod—God bless your true heart!—take your hands off me. I am perfectly myself again. I am Elisha Stone once more. It is gone, that hideous darkness. I am calm and self-possessed, only I have the pent-up wrath of a mill-dam when I see that man's foul wrong to us all."

"Heaven knows, I believe him, father," responded Horace, and tears were beginning to streak down his dusty cheeks. "We haven't seen that appearance in his eyes for many a day." And he wrung my hand, but held it fast in both of his.

The elder shook his head dubiously. "I fear it will not last. This excitement is bad. But there she comes," said he, turning his head towards the path through which Mary Holyoke and his good wife had taken their way to come to us.

"Yes," I protested; "there she comes, God's good angel! It is such as she, and this dear family here, Mr. Littlewood, which keep man's faith in God that it fly not up from the earth like frightened larks that never mean to return. But you, man, you robber, with whining cant, you are like—I will say it, for you are too old to grapple with—you are like a crow that feeds on the carcasses which others have slain. Your 'amens' sound to me like 'caw, caw, caw.' Now, go get into your vehicle while you may." I walked near enough to enforce my order on the next instant.

"Why, why, dan-net!" exclaimed Littlewood, stepping back. "The boy must go to the asylum, elder?" he whispered, with a faint laugh; and yet there were both anger and fear in the sound.

"Go!" I insisted, striving—like Samson, all my strength returning—to free my hand from Horace's fetter. I sprang a step or two forward as I loosed my hand. Mr. Littlewood went through that barway like a jumping-jack on a pole at the county fair, and tumbled with a sprawl on his wagon-seat. Grasping the reins, he whipped up and drove away. I stood and watched him a moment, until a few rods farther up the highway he turned in at the granite gateway of what had been once my home.

"Does Cynthia live there?" I demanded.

"Don't tell him," protested the elder, with a quivering lip and uncertain tone.

"Hod?"—I turned to him to insist on a reply.

"I pray you not to cherish any anger against Cynthia," the boy answered. "We all see plainly enough now, even mother sees, where the girl has got her promptings and guidings for the course she has taken."

"Tell me, has she gotten possession? Is she married to that fellow, the singer?" I was relentless in my demand.

"Don't ask—don't think of our wrongs now, Elisha," exclaimed a woman's voice. I had felt her approach at my left much as, I suppose, a stone ledge must feel the advance of daybreak, though it has no eyes, for I had no eyes towards anything except that retreating vehicle in the highway.

But now I turned to greet Mary Holyoke. She pulled my folded arms apart, she clasped my great soiled knuckles with her long twining fingers of white.

"Elisha, my son"—this voice was that of that dear motherly soul Mrs. Parkridge, who was also at my side now—"we did indeed know that our Heavenly Father's love was loving kind long before this; but now that He has restored you, oh, how good He is!"

"Most gracious lady," I answered her, "my best friend's loving mother, I don't wonder that you can lead Horace with a touch of your finger. You are the nearest to a mother that I ever knew." I was in such a softened frame of mind that I stooped over the little creature, and just where the white hairs parted on her forehead I kissed her.

Beaming on me, she asked : "Mother, did you say, Elisha?—did you think of me as mother, child? I knew your mother, child! See—she sleeps yonder amid those graves of my own kin." Her thin trembling finger pointed away up the hill-side, where the white marble shone in her own private God's acre.

"My mother?"

"His mother?" echoed Mary.

"Elisha's mother?" chimed in Horace's deep voice.

"Yes, children," she resumed; "a fatherless, motherless little lad, I laid this lone boy in my cradle long ago. It was along this very road that the dying woman wandered. It was a weary night in harvest. I had seen her passing and repassing with her baby—you, Elisha—in her arms all the afternoon. As it grew dark she sank down by the stone gate-post of the Senator's driveway there. I could not endure the sight without helping, and went to her. She sat leaning her head against the granite. Her eyes were closed, her face was surpassingly beautiful. She was a large noble woman of five-and-thirty years. She wore rich garments, but they were all in tatters and travel-stained. Her hands were soft, and unused to hard labor, I am sure. She was dead, and you were sleeping in her embrace."

We younger people drank this all in with silent wonder. I saw at a glance that it was as much news to Horace and Mary as to me. Only the features of the two men, Mr. Holyoke and Elder Park-ridge, revealed recognition of the story. You may be sure that, for the moment, I could not speak.

"Her simple funeral was yonder at our own house," added the elder, fervently.

"And you reared the baby?" I at length got words to add, with unspeakable emotion.

"Yes."

After a further silence, when all this came fully upon me, and I had some measure of appreciation of its height and depth of meaning, I broke the sacred stillness, saying, "For that I ought to thank you, and I do, that you reared me. But more, I bless you that these kindly hands," taking hers in my own, "composed my mother for her burial. For that—oh, for that—anything! While I breathe will I hold myself a slave to do for you and yours." I kissed her good hands over and over again.

"Then obey me, will you?" she asked.

"Yes, foster-mother, I covenant before God I will always obey you."

"Then promise me that you will seek no revenges on the unhappy Mr. Littlewood, his daughter, or Mr. Felton."

I was not prepared for that—no, not for that. Yet I managed to say,

"I promise you. Only justice; I may seek justice?"

"No vengeance. Leave that to God."

"Yes, but justice." I was eager, no doubt.

"True, in due time I will help you to that. Perhaps the law will help you too."

"Now tell me more of my mother," I was quick to demand.

"Elisha, what if my telling you of your mother were to rob Horace of his mother?"

This quite took my breath away. After a moment I answered, "I can't understand you, dear lady."

"Horace is passing through the severest trial of his life," she resumed. "If I were to die and be at rest—however sweet and grateful, oh, Heaven, that would be, so long have I carried this burden —if I were to die, the boy would break away from all good. It is for me that he stays here on the farm, for my sake that he has turned his back on the evil ways that he learned in the great cities."

"Yes, yes," I interposed; "but my mother, how does your life depend on your keeping from me what you know of her?"

"Because"—I couldn't bear what would come to my own if justice were just now done to the guilty. I couldn't bear it and live! But it shall come; justice a little later. Wait until I am a little nearer to my natural limit of life! For Horace's sake will you not wait and let me live?"

"A thousand years, if need be," answered I. "Let anything happen to me, it is all the same, if nothing evil happens to you. I loved you all before; but now, for what you have told me of your deed to her who sleeps yonder, I would give my life for you and yours!"

Just then the long winding call of the dinner-horn, blown by the hired girl from yonder farmhouse stoop, echoed in the sultry air. It was a most unpoetic and abrupt breaking-in on a scene the most intense in all my life thus far. I can feel it yet—the cooling splash of that water on my burning cheeks.

I did not trust myself to go till evening. I remember that after dinner I got Mrs. Parkridge to describe particularly to me the location of my mother's mound on the hill there. Then I went back to my work in the furrow. But when we had done milking, just about sunset, I started off

9

in a straight walk back of the barns, and went to stand by that grave.

I have heard that all men honor such a spot, but it is not so. Here all about me were neglected mounds. Had these sleepers no children? Oh, how it gnawed my heart out to see the mound sunken, overgrown with wild grasses, and all unmarked! I stooped down and reaped away the grasses with my fingers, I smoothed and caressed the turf till it was clean-shaven as a rich man's lawn, and I watered the stubble with my tears. I brought fresh earth in my hands, holding the cold soil against my breast as I did it. I fashioned the grave with these hands over my mother. I would have done all this, if I had had to carry the earth a thousand miles. I had little money, but I vowed a headstone for the next sweet Sunday. It should be there by Sunday, when next the people came to walk there. I would sell clothing if Fordham, the stone-cutter, would not trust me. I would give my wages that I must have earned. I had such a crushing sense of shame upon me, to think of it—my mother in an unmarked grave!

When it was all done as best I could do, then I stood with folded arms over it, the sunset warming me till it slipped from the mound and from me. She was beautiful, they told me. I had no faintest memory of her face. She held me in her fainting arms, alone and desolate herself, and sheltered me from the blazing harvest sun as we crouched at the very gates of my future home. My big bony frame shook with the emotions that took hold on me. All the childlike in me, which it is taught must return again to every man who enters into the kingdom of heaven, got mastery over the man. I flung myself down and cried like a child. I prayed as I wept — prayed for my rights on earth, for a home, and for Mary. When at length I rose up, I went and told Horace Parkridge that tears had furnished what laughter only begun. I was once more a man among men.

CHAPTER IX

THE next morning, as we rose from the breakfast-table, Mary said to me, "Elisha, walk along towards the school-house with me."

"You are the teacher this term, then, I take it," I answered.

"Yes ; that seemed to be necessary, and I am very thankful that I can earn the money. Come ; I want to talk with you on the way."

"Certainly ; I am to be planting corn there in the field this side of the school-house," I answered. Shouldering my hoe, we started off together. We went out into the highway on the north, and before much more was said were fairly opposite the entrance to my property. I still thought of it as my property, for by rights it was mine.

"The noble old house is always majestic in the morning light," I remarked, somewhat sadly. Always now I seemed to see my mother crouching there in her beauty and sorrow.

"Always beautiful," echoed Mary, cheerily. "Everything is beautiful on such a morning as this to an innocent and honest heart, Elisha." Then, after a brief silence, she asked, with much more meaning than her words expressed, "The world appears bright to you, does it not, this glorious morning?"

Instead of answering, I said, "Do you fear for me, then?"

"No; I don't fear for you, I trust for you." Yet I should have read her fear, despite her assurance.

"I am well once more," I insisted, "be sure of it. I didn't sleep last night. I came out here and walked all about old Bosworth Place, and took my resolve anew. You don't expect me to submit while there is a breath of life in me to this miserable wrong, this robbery?"

"No; I am sure that would not be manly; but—"

"Hear me, Mary"—I spoke with gathering earnestness—"many things unspeakably sad have transpired since we sang that hymn together in the town-hall at the singing-school. I am now a defrauded and penniless man, but I am more certain than ever that you love me."

"Elisha!"—but the rich blood was flushing her neck and cheeks.

"Yes; and we might marry—"

"If"—and she was silent.

"If what, you precious girl?"

"Provided I do confess that I do love you more than any mortal, may I tell you what I mean by—if?"

I stopped her in the path. She did not now throw my arm away—a caress that I had not given her since we were romping children together on the farm.

"Yes ; say anything you wish, my girl."

"If, then, Elisha Stone, you were sure of your-self. It has been a terrible malady."

How hard it was to hear that no one can know but he who has once passed under the shadow of a mental malady. It is fearful! It is a ghost that haunts you from morning to evening with the awful menace of some sudden return. Your friends do not return to confidence. You read their apprehension in their eager questions, in their searching glances, in their sudden starts and turnings towards you. You reach the very depths when you detect that your dearest kin are afraid to be left alone with you. No; there is a deeper depth still: it is your own con-scious struggle to appear calm that you may vin-dicate yourself, to do no unnatural thing, to give no free rein to such indignation as great provocations like mine would naturally excite in other men, lest you should be judged mad again.

"Did I not show my self-control, Mary, when I last night walked all about the old house by such light as a quarter-moon bestowed, patted my old dog on the head—he knew me and licked my hands—gazed into my own windows, behind which I had dreamed you would sit, and saw the piled furniture of another, new house-keeping, and yet did not rage over that sight of the boxes and bales of Cynthia Littlewood's new elegance on the front stoop ?"

"Perhaps even yet they will never be married," mused Mary.

"I think it is tolerably certain now," I laughed in a hard way. "Felton is opening the new village store that he has set up on her money, is he not?"

"You surprise me, Elisha. Who told you all this news?"

"Peleg, the faithful old soul."

"Then you found him on the old place last night?"

"Certainly, and devoted as ever. He was at first shy of me, but when he saw that I was myself again he almost bowed down to me. He says the wedding is to be in two weeks. Felton divides his time between the new store and his new home. There he is now, crossing the east wheatfield among the stubble."

She searched me with her glances as I was gazing at the approaching man. Then she added this test:

"Yes, I see that is Felton. And what if I told you that he has frequently been at the school-house of late?"

I could not endure it. I felt that I should grapple the man if we met, but I also knew that the girl was putting me to the proof. I turned to the wall, put my hand on the rail above the stone, and vaulted into the cornfield without a word to go to work.

"Elisha Stone?"

"I do not distrust you, Mary, but really here is where the rows begin, and I may as well confess that I cannot trust myself to meet that man here. Elsewhere; let it be elsewhere. I am arranging my plans—I am not afraid to meet him, but not here. Something might happen. It is nearly nine o'clock, Mary."

I fell furiously at work at the planting, when Felton sprang on the bars at the other side of the highway shouting out:

"Good-morning, Miss Mary; I have come to say good-byes."

"Why, sir?" she responded, turning upon him in a half-frightened way.

"I am going to war. When I return I will be Governor." At the same time he threw off a light outer garment, and there he stood, an apparition, a soldier in full uniform, sword at side. Only a painter could do justice to that moment: to the handsome lady, on whose astonished features dislike thawed away in dawning admiration; to the fluttering groups of school-children, stopped all agog and hardly daring to chirp their unbounded amazement; and to my homely self, leaning on my hoe, and wondering if I were in possession of my senses.

"Yes, sweet lady"— advancing, while the sword, a real sword, shining brightly, clanked as he walked — "the great war for the Union is on you know. We fight for glory and the nation's life. You have read all the news, of course, these days?"

He utterly ignored me, as time and the great world's mighty history had surely also done of late. Those mighty events of the winter of '61 had hardly a faint belonging to my life.

"But—but—your wedding, sir."

That Mary would condescend to speak to him at all showed me how much this vast war theme must have occupied everybody's attention. I also recalled the Holyokes' intense patriotism. That this fellow would actually offer himself to fight for his country had instantly redeemed him to a certain degree, so that this pure-hearted girl would address him words of courteous reply.

"My wedding? Well, it must wait. Miss Cynthia and I have almost had a quarrel," pulling out his sword an inch or two, and thrusting it back with a tiny clang.

"Indeed," quite coolly Mary replied. Then she offered to go on with her children, who flew towards her.

"Yes," he interposed; "Heaven only knows, Miss Holyoke, what will transpire while I am away on the field of proud adventure," and he stepped before her like a cavalier. "I go at once. I have put some money into the regiment, and shall go as colonel. Of course, being an educated man, I could not think of serving in the ranks. The position itself might be considered highly gratifying to any gentleman. At my store

a company is forming to-night, which will be a
part of my regiment. I have put some money
into that also."

"Money, Mr. Felton?" objected Mary, with a
disdainful toss of her head.

"Oh, I know what you refer to," he fenced.
"To be sure, the Littlewoods have profited by
my legal acumen, and have paid me large fees.
I regard it in the light of fees."

"Sir, I do not wish to discuss these matters
with you," answered Mary. "Quite likely we
shall not meet again ; but we simple country-
folks, may I be allowed to say, consider that you
owe your store—and now, you confess, your ability
to get official position — to Cynthia Littlewood's
money ; and ill-gotten gains of hers they are, too."

"Sweet lady, hear me," resumed he, removing
the jaunty military cap by the visor and dropping
it upon the shoulder, where an eagle gleamed
upon the strap, "shall I reward Cynthia by mar-
rying without loving her?"

Mary's brown eyes simply stared at him.

"And shall I not be permitted, even for the
last time, probably, to protest to you that I would
put my honors—and they may be many before
my hairs are gray—all my success at your feet?
Think of it!—if I live, if I return to this village,
if I enter the political arena, laying aside the
sword, what might I not hope for amid these
rustics ? Let me at least dream, upon the strick-
en field, of you with some slight hope."

To write it down as I do now makes such boasting seem incredible, yet it was not by any means disgusting to hear him say it in his fine way.

"Elisha!" The words were those of alarm. I bounded across that fence like a deer. The fellow, seeing me advance, actually drew his weapon with a fencer's skill. I raised my hoe, and in a moment more I think I could have brained him, when he suddenly bethought himself, and hissed, speaking to himself:

"Fie!—to fight with an imbecile!" and he lowered his sword.

The wrath of weeks swelled within me. My arm throbbed with pain as I poised the hoe in air. But that word "imbecile," and Mary's cry, "Heaven help us!" was enough. I was to prove to the girl that I was a strong man, as strong as the strongest—that I was no dangerous monomaniac. And how I thanked God, after an instant of second thought, for this opportunity of showing my self-control. I lowered the hoe into the dust, and said, calmly:

"Arthur Alfred Felton, allow this lady to pass on!"

"Good-bye, Miss Holyoke," he said, in a courtly way at once, ignoring me again, though I saw that he could not believe his senses when I did not rave like a madman. "I wanted to have said more," he added. "I can—I have the desire, indeed—to reinstate your father in his old home—"

"Come, Elisha," Mary said, shuddering as she drew near to me.

"And I beg of you," Felton flung after us, "not to take too seriously what I said about my quarrel with the Littlewood lass. If you tell her what I have confessed to you she will not believe you."

"What do you say, Mary?" I asked, as the military form disappeared over the rail-fence and behind the blackberry-bushes.

"I fear he is right. There seems to be a fatality in his power over her. But this is the forks of the road with her—that is, when we inform her of what he has this day said;" and she lapsed into deep thought. His parting words seemed to linger on the summer air—"If you tell her what I have confessed to you she will not believe you." Perhaps the man was right. At any rate, he had safely hedged, and so parted from us.

Mary, walking on to the school, gathered her children to order, and when they had been fairly started upon their tasks she sat down with me on the broad stone door-step of the porch. She could there keep an eye upon her little brood, and also give me attention. She narrated to me with glowing eloquence all the stirring events in our national life which had occurred in the last few weeks. It was a lucid, sympathetic, and graphic history. When she had concluded she added:

"And now, my brave knight, I congratulate you on the possession of yourself again, for none but a sound heart and steady head could have kept itself as you did a few moments ago under such terrific provocation."

"Then," I answered, rising to my feet with expectancy, "will you trust yourself to marry me now, or shall I also enlist first and help my countrymen mow this heavy swath?"

"They will not take you for your country's service yet," she answered. "Mr. Littlewood has slandered you all through the town, and means even worse things for you possibly. You must stay and outwit him. You must prove yourself to be yourself once more. Horace will go, for he is a broken-hearted man."

"And I promised, did I not, to do anything in the world for the little mother who served my mother at the last? You are right: some one must care for her, and the elder is not strong. It may be that if Horace goes it will kill his mother. Have you really heard Hod say whether he was going or not?"

I dreaded to hear her reply. Under the glowing history of public events from this fair narrator's lips I had become excited to the highest pitch. To go — to escape these small flies of miseries that buzzed about one in the country-side — to do the manly, heroic thing, and that, too, in any possible position: as a mere musket-carrier, if necessary—these were my impulses.

"Yes; speaking of Horace," Mary answered, "it

has been all talked over. Horace is going to enlist
to-night at the Union store."

This was weighty news. It was hard to realize.

It came over me like a revelation after a moment more of thought—for we interspersed our
conversation with long pauses of serious medita-
tion—the wisest, manliest thing, the sudden opening of duty, which comes to all men, I believe, at
times, like a sudden flash of light on a dark path.
"Mary Holyoke, if I stay here our marriage must
wait also. I could die for you, as you know, but
I could not ask you to lower your high standard
of what you think is manly and womanly. It
would not do for us to be happy at home while
he whom we love has gone to suffer, and he whom
we have reason to despise is masquerading also as
a hero in behalf of our country."

"Oh, you great brave loyal heart, Heaven bless
you!" she answered. "I do thank you for saying
that. I am glad that you should have said it first,
and without promptings from me. No, indeed, we
could not take each other now, seeking our own
happiness selfishly, while I am under Horace's
roof and my father and mother are the guests of
their benevolence."

She arose, putting out her hands as a clasp on
my folded arms. I saw the woman's devotion for
the man of her choice in her long and restful gaze.
She added:

"Now, then, can you take up this plain, inglori-

ous task among us sorrowing women and old people, and wait?"

"I will, God helping me," I answered. And,
saying that, I started back to my work in the
field, while Mary entered the school-room. How
little we knew in this play of youthful enthusi-
asm and heroism what a world of risk we as-
sumed. We had no adequate understanding of
the many things that might happen between the
present and the moment of our glad union, the
wedding-day which seemed then not far away.

CHAPTER X

"Whom will you have for captain, men?" Colonel Felton was standing on a dais by the end of his little private office in the Union store. Cynthia was caged within the wire fencing, leaning an elbow on the open ledger; but her eyes were on the colonel, not on the page of accounts. She wore a hat and coat, as if she had just come in from driving. Her eyes showed traces of weeping and her face was flushed. The yellow lamplight from over her head, fighting with the twilight of the summer evening, lent her face deep lines that did not belong there; or else she was angry, and passion had scarred her features.

The ancient rambling room of the country store was capable of accommodating perhaps two-score men; but a hundred were now trying to get in, or were already crammed within its narrow quarters, when Horace and I came up.

"Open the doors and throw up the windows," cried Felton; "that will give us the piazza, also."

This building had for years been the very heart of the village. All its tide of life beat in and out here with every impulse of excitement, of pleasure, of gossip, of buying and selling, of politics and religion, sooner or later. Everybody came here for business or for loitering.

"I ain't nothin' on swappin' hosses to - night, Isik," I overheard one farmer say to another.

"'Pears like politiks is throbbin' with a pooty quick pulse. Some on us has got to go an' fight," was the comment of a second man.

"D'yer see th' new sign?" was wise old farmer Kipling's reply to them both. I turned and saw that it was my next-door neighbor on our road. "He's rubbed out Maher Ashe's letterin', what's ben thar fifty year; but ye k'n see 'em in shadder, as if the dead old man's ghost was peepin' through to see what his successor's doin'—ARTHUR ALFRED FELTON, showin' bright in new gold, but th' old letters dodgin' raound. They say that old Ashe's heirs will get fifty thousan' dollars when th' old man's 'state 's settled."

"New paint an' fixin's 's all well 'nuff, neighbor, but this young daown-country feller can't be no sech reg'lar father 'n Isr'el 's Maher was. No doubt Maher's gone to a better place, though." And my neighbor seated himself on the counter while he lighted his pipe.

"Where's he hid his codfish?" asked Job Stout, whose open jack-knife blade was ready in his hand for the accustomed pickings.

"Guess it's gone after the sugar barrel. Vum ter Moses, but that ain't no way ter get trade," growled Peleg Rumney.

"An' th' plug terbaccer's skipped in back, too,"
was the further comment of Kipling, whose empty pipe was twirling in his fingers. "Mighty
stric'ly bizness, ain't he, on Littlewood's money?"

" 'Tain't Littlewood's money; it's Cynthy's."

"Wa'al; but it's the deacon's idees of savin', jist
the same."

"He'll save th' money, won't he," sneered another, "powerful smart sight! Then that's th'
cunnel's uniform, is it?" glancing up at Felton,
who stood fully revealed on the dais. "Don't
that beat Cunnel Robbins's old-fashioned honest
Vermont uniforms all ter thunder? Cost a dozen
of Cynthy's sheep, I bet yer."

"But he's cuttin' a swath," growled Jack Stout.

It was evident that Felton had lost standing in
the estimation of my neighbors, and also equally
evident that Deacon Littlewood was decidedly
unpopular with our honest farmers, who had kept
fully informed of his recent sharp practices for
the gaining of extra acres. On the other hand,
there was a searching look of pity and questioning in every man's face that met me, which seemed
to be in kindly contrast. Horace and I kept together and wedged our way in and in, closer to
the counter, where, at Cynthia's right, young
Charlie Lane, a school-boy, with a clear ringing
voice, was reading to the assembled crowd the
New York Tribune and the *Boston Journal.*
There was some horse-play and jesting, and an
occasional hurrah over a passage or two in the

speech of our Congressman ; but, for the most
part, a deep seriousness held the compact mass of
countrymen in silence.

"Whom will you name, gentlemen ?" shouted
Felton again, as the reader paused to turn his
paper. "We have eighty-three names of Northbrook boys on the roll," holding it up, "all these
—a nomenclature of great names." He sounded
forth that swelling word with proud impressive-
ness.

"What 'n tarnation 's that ?" grunted Tom Calkins.

Unmindful of the saucy interruption, Felton
went on, "Calkins, I think you would make a
good captain."

"Hod Parkridge's a handsomer boy to be
dressed up in regimentals. Besides, he's been in
a blue coat before."

"Yes ; Parkridge ! Parkridge !" resounded
through the room.

"But, gentlemen—"

"Parkridge — the sailor — Parkridge — Hod
Parkridge !" a perfect storm of it.

"I say, gentlemen," angrily interposed Felton
again, "I am to be the colonel of this regiment.
Northbrook only furnishes one company."

"What of that ? You don't own us."

The colonel's face grew paler. "But there are
reasons why it might not be altogether agreeable
to me, as the superior officer, to have Mr. Parkridge—"

"Yes, I should say so," came derisively from a man sitting astride a crockery crate in the corner; at which many laughed, and the colonel grew a trifle paler still.

"Hod, take it," I urged, in under-tone, as I saw him making ready to protest. "Don't you see that it is only his money at the capital that has bought him the place, and he will resign in no time? You will be in the line of promotion. You, old boy, will come back a colonel of the — Vermont."

Cynthia overheard me, for in the movement and wedging of the crowd we had now been pressed up very near to the bookkeeper's cage. She flashed her black eyes on him. As yet she had not given him any sign of recognition, but already I could see her comparing him with her colonel.

"Read all the names and let us vote," came from a man who had mounted the box-stove and was swinging his straw hat in the air till it touched the low ceiling. The cry was taken up and became a shout. Felton heard it become a roar, and still refused to yield, and began making up the enlistment roll into a cylinder in his hand. The roar became a perfect babel.

"Here, let us vote. Parkridge, Parkridge for captain from Northbrook!" Everybody was saying it.

With an angry toss Felton flung the roll down on the desk before Cynthia. We overheard him spit it out:

"Curses on these bucolics! They mean to shove this fellow into my regiment as captain. Cynthia, there is no help for it. You will have to read, and let them vote."

Cynthia was almost at the point of weeping with the excitement. How surpassingly beautiful she was, as I remember her then! The girl was wretchedly unhappy. I was sure of it. Did she not say it in the woods, that she only wanted to be happy? Turning towards Horace, with an impulsive quiver, there was the faintest flavor of old-time recognition in her tones as she asked:

"Have you ever enlisted, Horace?" That was just enough, the mere trace of any interest in him lingering in her tone, and he yielded in a moment.

"Yes; this forenoon," he answered, warmly. That was all, and commonplace enough, you would say. But the sound of his voice, which she had not so much as heard for weeks, must have struck some old chord in the girl's heart. Perhaps her quarrel with Felton had prepared the way. And perhaps, too, nature made these twain for each other.

"And as a private, too?" She beamed it on the paper, and said it to the page, not to him, and yet she knew, of course, that he would hear. "*You* have not bought *your* honors, but you shall have them just the same."

I am sure of this much, that she meant to use this nobility of his as a whip over her high-stepper,

for she spoke the last part of her sentence loud
enough for Felton also to hear it. He did hear it,
and answered her with a sarcastic smile of one
who felt secure in his mastery. She was piqued
by his expression, and began reading the names
promptly in a silvery ringing tone. From A to
Y, voice after voice, hoarse voices, clear voices,
boyish voices, manly voices, answering, "Parkridge "—" Hod "—" Hod Parkridge "—" the sail-
or "—" the preacher's boy." At least seventy-
nine names present and voting, as I kept the tally
on a piece of wrapping-paper, which lies before me
now as I write about it, all for Horace.

"I will not announce it," growled Felton in
low tones to Cynthia.

"I will," I answered, reaching my hand for the
tally.

" Why, 'Lish Stone," exclaimed Cynthia, for the
first time noticing me, " are you here? Are you
well? Ought you to be here?" But she gave
me the paper on which she had the tally nevertheless. I called for silence, and as it was coming
slowly over the uproarious crowd Cynthia remarked, in plainly audible words, leaning towards
the wicket till her red lips almost touched Horace's ear :

"I am glad, brave man—I am glad for you. I
have not forgotten how handsome you used to
look in your sailor's uniform."

" In the happier days, Cynthia," the boy turned
to say, scarce allowing her to finish her sentence

—"before he came between us. Are you going to marry him? Tell me, for I shall not likely see you again, if that is the case. Is it not God's providence, which father tells us so much about, that is just now in season separating you from him?"

"Don't ask me now," she answered. "I am coming over to your house to-morrow to say good-bye."

Felton, whose attention had been momentarily attracted to another part of the room, managed to catch the mere ends of this conversation, and he glowered on her, though he could not quite terrorize her into silence. This seemed to anger him as she went on whispering.

"The result is," I cried to the crowd, "that Horace Parkridge is elected captain of Company C of — Regiment of Vermont Volunteers."

Then the cheers, the hats in air, hurrah on hurrah, and anything and everything that could be thrown up to the low ceiling flung against it to the storm of cheers; while out on the stoop anything and everything that could be thrown up was tossed with deafening huzzas towards the darkening summer sky. These men of the fields are phlegmatic until a great excitement seizes on them, then they are wilder, more irresistible, than any other people, as runaway oxen are far more destructive when they get started than runaway horses.

"What do you want of him?" demanded Felton, as he slipped over through the gateway to Cynthia's side.

She drew back. "What I please, sir."

"How is that, my lady, since you are wearing my ring?"

"Here!" she flung back at him, snatching the ring from her finger. But then she paused. "Why should I? My money bought it."

I overheard this; but of course the crowd did not, for cheer on cheer was still being flung against the ceiling, and cheer on cheer broke out beyond the doors, mingled with a cry:

"There's his father and mother—the dear old parson and Mother Parkridge—driving up!"

The uproar prevented my hearing the further conversation of Felton and Cynthia after her home thrust. The crowd prevented Horace and me moving had we wished. The boy, seeing a gleam of hope in Cynthia's sudden attempt at rebellion from the long fatal spell which the singer had thrown over her, whispered to me,

"'Lish, lay hold!" And he knit his fingers into the wire fencing. He was like a tiger. A moment more and he would have torn a way to the girl's side and her defending. But just at that moment the crowd, with the fickle movements of a throng, took him up bodily on their shoulders with a yell of adulation, and began passing him out over their heads that he might greet his parents and receive their blessings. It was out there in front of the store, in the dim twilight of that May evening, that over the head of his son, who stood at the carriage-wheel, the elder made that great war speech. Everybody in Northbrook has heard of it. Its traditions live still in all the country-side.

Felton took advantage of the diverted attention of the people to manage this troublesome situation with Cynthia.

"I ask your forgiveness." It came as quick as shadows flit.

"I don't know whether I will give it to you or not," she answered.

"But all the crowd are turned away from us," he went on. "Don't disgrace me by manifesting our quarrel so unmistakably to these people who know us."

"You are not sincere," she responded. "I have been half persuaded for some weeks that I ought to tell you so, even if we parted."

"Do you wish to break the engagement—to ruin one whom you hold in your power?" he pleaded. Then he seemed to me to bethink himself of another weapon, for he exclaimed, somewhat sternly, "I am his colonel." Now his features manifested unmistakably his malevolence as he went on: "Do I not know that you have small love for me of late? Were it not for the deacon, your father, you would have broken this engagement when I resolved to put my own personal happiness second to the great call of my suffering country's need, adjourning the wedding."

"Indeed !—the call of your suffering country, colonel and future Governor!" She laughed scornfully.

"Then we part so?" And now his anger was wholly unmasked. "I am his colonel," with a nod of his head towards Horace out-of-doors. "Yes; I will confess that your money made it possible for me to raise this regiment. He has a company in my regiment. I will put him where death is falling thick enough to mow grass."

As he spoke to her I had a new illustration of his spell over her by the use he made of his voice. He was an orator. He could throw into the eye, the features, and most of all the voice, the very soul of meaning. Under his threat the girl quailed, starting back, crying:

"Can you, indeed, do that? Oh, I suppose you can. We girls know nothing of war. Spare him, spare him, and I will replace the ring. I do not love him." And she fairly pleaded with the man for a return to his amiable mood.

"Very well," he said, "you do not love me, but you shall not ruin me," and he smiled with a self-satisfied air of one who was sure of his victory.

"Arthur Alfred Felton"—I spoke it hotly; I could have shaken down the frail partition that separated us as I saw his abuse of the girl—"I will pin you to the wall, and staple your throat with my fingers, if you push the girl further with your terrors!"

"You!" He gave a startled stare; I knew

what it meant. In another instant he would alarm the crowd outside by proclaiming me a madman. "Are you at large yet? I had forgotten that I had seen you here," he added.

Again my penalty was on me. I turned from him and went out, and with an iron composure which surprises me now as I recall it. Does any one wonder how I was able to keep myself? Think of Mary's God and her prayers. I found myself a little later hurrying over to my lawyer's office, repeating the expressions of a prayer as I walked along, and as I stood upon the door-step of his office—the prayers that I had often heard her use for self-control. There is something in this calling upon God. Whoever reads this, let me assure you, however your brain may whirl with intense passion at times, there is something in prayer that can hold a man. I remember, moreover, that I thought of Ashael Keep's bare cobweb-strung office as a good place to cool off an angry man's fever.

The little lawyer pulled down his feet from the window-sill as I entered. He had been watching composedly from his office windows the bonfire on the common that the enthusiastic villagers had now set blazing. That accounted for the red in his usually pale face. War or peace, it was all the same to the shrewd yet surely honest old bachelor, who seemed to neither love nor hate— Ashael Keep. But even he had managed to get some heat in his blood over my own personal

wrong, for catching sight of me he sprang up
and said:

"My boy, glad of it," and he extended his little hand, "glad you are all right — knew you
would be — ain't goin' to war, are you? Hod's
goin'—you'll have to stay an' airn bread for the
folks up there, and give 'em care. Too bad! No
glory for you! Ha, ha! No case at Nashua
against the doctor, either, who gave you the war-
ranty deed on the Senator's place. Bad-luck, boy.
He died a month ago. No estate. Wuthless son
in Chicago had spent all he had. Come in and set
down. That sickness o' yours been very unfortunate. Lots o' things happened sence you were
sick. Been expectin' you every hour sence I heard
you'd become yourself again."

"But," I said, taking a chair, after all this out-
burst of the usually reticent man, "if I have no
case against the doctor, I certainly have against
Deacon Littlewood for defamation of character."

"Yes, sir-ee, go in! It's time that man was
brought to book."

"And since there is a just Ruler on high, I
must have a case in a righteous court with regard to my property, if I could only patch it together."

The man shook his head and tilted back in his
chair.

"Keep, see here, where is Mrs. Cark?" I demanded, leaning towards him, and going directly

to the marrow of the errand that I had really had in mind for the last forty-eight hours.

"Up there taking care of the Bosworth place, I suppose," he answered, gnawing his thumbs.

"Who is she?"

"Who? You ought to know. What's up?" And he began to show interest and hope in my case at once.

"I found her there when I went there, and I kept her, expecting that I would be rid of her in some charitable way when Mary came to live with me. Now, see here, Keep, that woman must know something about my childhood; and moreover Mrs. Parkridge, I discover, knew who my mother was. Mrs. Parkridge knows something about Cynthia's nativity and her childhood days."

The little lawyer bit his thumbs in silence.

I waited a time, while the bonfire's glow flashed higher just in front of the liberty pole, not ten rods from the window, watching the lawyer's face. It seemed a very long time, and I had shot out pretty much all that I had in my pouch. It was just to say these few simple things that I had lain awake half the night resolving upon this errand to the lawyer, but it seemed to have made comparatively little impression upon him. He gnawed the corner of his lip and his thumbs, but made me no reply.

While we were gazing out of the window Elder Parkridge moved his horse and buggy out from the crowd, where he had been speaking.

Horace brought the dear little mother along from
Widow Hopewell's millinery and dress - making
shop, which was next house in the corner of the
lot to the south. The red light flashed on the
group.

"My duty is, Mary says, to care for them while
he is gone to be a hero," I remarked to Keep.

"Your duty is to follow out *that!*" and the
lawyer let his tilted chair drop with a crash to
all fours, and quick as a hound upon the scent,
with hand and head thrust forward, he pointed
out of the window towards this group of people.

There, side by side in the fitful flashes of the
light, stood two women — the woman whom all
the township loved, and the woman whom not a
soul of us in the township ever knew much about
or cared much about—Mrs. Parkridge and Mrs.
Cark. Mrs. Cark was speaking to Mrs. Parkridge.
I do not remember that I ever saw them standing
side by side before, or, if I had, it was not in silent
picturing like this. Two sisters may resemble each
other ever so closely in feature and form, but the
moment they speak the contrast of soul is shown.
Here, however, in silence the two women stood up
for our observation.

"How much alike they look!" exclaimed the
lawyer. The keen perception and the quick rea-
soning of that attorney has not ceased to be an
astonishment to me to this day.

CHAPTER XI

"I wish it were any other day but Sunday that I am to say good-bye," said Horace, mournfully. How quickly we did things those times ! Elected captain on Thursday night, off to the war on Sunday.

"But what a gorgeous day for our hero," Mary Holyoke broke the silence for us all. "The valley was never so lovely ! What a vision of the sleeping mountains ! That sheen on the lake, the miles on miles of farms, all bathed in the sacred Sabbath repose !" We were a family group on the elder's piazza.

"Thank you, dear heart," said Horace, brightening up. "You, at least, could not keep silence any longer without trying to say a word of cheer." And he forced a laugh.

"We need not whip up our smiles, my boy, as if there was nothing to smile about," remarked the elder. "We have ever so much to be thankful for. You go on Heaven's own errand—much to be thankful for. We are all in good health," and then his vision of blessings seemed suddenly to have been foreshortened, for he did not recount any added ones in sight.

"You remind me, father," at length Hod remarked, " of Peleg Rumney's errand over here this morning. He had evidently been repairing the harness. He had an old horse-collar on his arm. 'I vum, Mr. Horace,' said he, 'that's a good collar if only Miss Cynthy 'd hev a harness made to 't.' "

"Speakin' of Cynthia, there she comes to bid you good-bye," quavered in the voice of Mr. Holyoke feebly from his seat on the doorstep.

"I sh'd think sh'd want to come here," protested Mrs. Holyoke, with a sigh, as she sat just behind the veranda trellis and hidden from sight. At the thought of Cynthia's approach she drew herself still further in hiding towards the farmhouse wall.

"Let's all be gracious and forgiving on my son's last day at the homestead," urged Horace's mother, rising from her chair and walking down towards the well-curb to be ready to receive her guest.

"I felt sure she would come here, Hod," I said, rising from the grass, where I had thrown myself beside Horace. We had been snipping the dandelions that starred the little lawn. When we rose up, Mary, all in white, tripped down the steps to us, took three or four dandelions from my hand, and began to fasten them on the blue field of Horace's uniform.

"I will keep them, you good angel to us all," he said, submitting. " They shall outlast these brass honors about which you pin them, though they are so frail."

"I dare say that it is the brass and blue she has come over here to see and compare;" ungraciously Mrs. Holyoke flung this out through the vines.

"Compare whom with whom, and what with what?" asked Horace.

"Why, her colonel, of course, in his uniform compared with the captain in his uniform," the unhappy lady sent him back reply.

"Her colonel, indeed, Hod," I said, slapping him on the shoulder. "Remember what I told you of the last end of the fracas down in the store."

The fellow flushed, and the memory brightened his countenance as no effort on his part to be cheerful had yet done. We walked down to the block that stood by the fence, and he helped Cynthia to alight.

"I thought I ought," she said, as she gave her foot to his hand and sprang to the ground. "Do you go soon?"

"In about an hour," he responded. Then followed greetings more or less cordial all round.

"Oh, it seems just horrid !" exclaimed the tall, dark girl, clutching her riding-habit with a graceful fling, and managing to put herself beside Horace—"dreadful, dreadful, to think how such fine - looking men as are going out of the valley may suffer and be abused before they are returned

11

to us again. I am simply too unhappy to live
any longer !"

" Only our gracious Father on high can help us
to endure all these things that it is our duty to
endure," fell from Mrs. Parkridge's lips and
mingled with her " good - afternoon." It sounded
like music, there was so much genuine faith in her
tone.

" Very kind of you to come over," interrupted
the elder, as he strode along over to the grass-
plot, holding out his tremendous hand. The usual cheerfulness with which he greeted everybody
was gone from his tone. " Mother," he said, taking his wife by the arm, " the boy's bag is on
the kitchen table for your last lookin' and tuckin'
in," and very abruptly led her back towards the
house.

" I am going to drive you down to the train,
Hod," I volunteered, seeing that he wanted to be
alone with Cynthia, " so I'd best go and harness
up."

The pair, thus left to themselves, strolled down
by the garden gate, and sat for twenty minutes
of the last precious hour that the boy was to have
with us on the bench under the elm. What was
said I never knew. They were conversing earnestly. They rose up and walked over to the maple at the end of the path ; then they paced back
and forth. I watched all this from the stable as
I was making ready.

The elder finally came over to the carriage-

house, and, with a choking voice, said: "'Lish,
drive up; that'll break her off. 'Tain't no good,
anyway. God defend the boy if he goes off this
time with a sore heart and no hope of the handsome gal! But I'm afraid, I'm afraid. Then, too,
I'm afraid his mother won't outlive it. Heavenly
Father, how hard Thou art! He's our only one.
'Lish, what have I said? No, God is not hard;
He is good. Forgive me, kind Heaven! It's terrible hard, though. I say, 'Lish,"—and then he
paused, as if to gather up his courage. I had
never seen the old man so rattle-brained. He was
always able to express himself with such homely
clearness. "'Lish," he resumed, "you haven't seen
anything?" And then he stopped and gnawed his
gray whisker, lifting it off from his breast and
tucking it between his lips.

"What is it, my dear sir?" I ventured, reverently, for he was shaking so that as he leaned on the
dasher of the buckboard the whole wagon felt the
thrill of his emotion.

"Well," he struggled it out, "you c'n understand—don't ever let him know I asked you—but
you haven't seen anything like his indulgin' in his
cups agin' sence he had his trouble with th' handsome witch yonder, have you?" And he empha-
sized each word of the sad question with a trembling forefinger pointing towards them.

"Why," I answered, "he stopped all that, out
of love for his mother."

"Yes—mother and the young lady," he replied.

"He said she never asked him to; but he told me she was such a pretty flyaway that if he had her he must be sober and strong, and be able to put the brakes on the team. That's 'fore anybody came between 'em."

"And that is as noble as it is true, elder. Heaven bless the boy!" I could not make up my mind to evade the truth further in my reply, and neither could I reassure him, the weary, anxious-hearted father. Heretofore in this story I have scarcely more than hinted at the waywardness and folly of Horace Parkridge's earlier years. And even now I cannot bring myself to put down on paper what I had lately seen of the spectre's return. So, after trying to turn the father's suspicions aside without telling a lie, I gathered up the lines and rattled out of the carriage-house.

The old preacher bowed, and, silently studying the ground, followed after me. "Shoo! shoo!" I heard him cry to the cackling geese behind me; "don't quack, quack our grief all over the neighborhood." There was something unspeakably sad as he talked to the geese.

As I drove up Cynthia was standing by the stile, about to mount. Horace was saying:

"I thank you for what you have told me. 'Lish heard what he said as well as you. No doubt death will be thick enough down there, but he must take his chances with the rest of us, or prove a poltroon."

"I do hope God will return you to us," she continued.

"You haven't answered my question," he persisted; "tell me that, and I will tell you whether I hope God will return me safely or not."

For what seemed a long time she made no reply. Then, with an impulsive little start and sigh, she said: "Well, I wear it still;" and she pulled off her glove for the first time, showing Felton's ring flashing in the sunlight.

"That is enough. Good-bye, and forever!" groaned Hod.

She hesitated a moment, bit her red lip, cast down her eyes until the black lashes rested on her cheeks, then pulled on the glove once more, and by his help was in the saddle without another word. Without further word to any of us, indeed, she wheeled her rearing colt, shot into the highway in a cloud of dust, and disappeared over the hill. He turned promptly to me.

"Well, 'Lish, time to go? Ah, she's gone! I don't care what becomes of her—she isn't worth a heart-throb! And yet she is—she might be. Wasn't she lovely, now, in appearance? But let her go—I say it anew;" and all this was uttered in low tones only for my ear. "I care not what becomes of her, or what becomes of Hod Parkridge!"

"Oh yes, you do," I protested; "for their sakes you care," pointing with the horsewhip towards the house guests and his parents, who were then approaching us.

Just then the clang of the great clock, standing so tall by the open bedroom window, sounded the hour.

"I was born in that room," remarked Horace.

"And you will sleep there many a night yet when your head is whiter than mine, so I pray for you, my only boy," said the elder, fairly shaking with his emotion, as he came up.

"Father, you have been a tender, loving parent to me. I have cost you many anxious prayers to Heaven."

"All of which are laid up on high," answered the mother, calmly. He did not find any word of fitting reply; his eyes alone answered her. Then in a desperate way he pushed past them, and walked up the path a little towards the house, saying to Mr. and Mrs. Holyoke:

"Good-bye, kind friends; and you, Mary, good-bye. Write me, won't you? I know 'Lish won't object to it. I shall want to see a woman's hand now and then. You and Mother Holyoke write me often. It will help me to be a decent man and a true soldier."

Mary had no reply upon her trembling lips as she bowed her promise, but she gave him her hand, and then returned with her parents to the stoop, leaving the young man alone with his father and mother. They seemed utterly to forget me, seated in the buckboard.

"Everything is in here," remarked his mother, as the elder lifted the small bag to the top of the stile. "Being an officer, you'll have some privilege of baggage, they say. You'll find—"

"Don't, mother, don't!" the boy pleaded, putting her hands back and gently forcing the bag to close.

"Well, well, I won't," wiping her eyes, and showing for the first time her relieving tears; "but you won't be careless of yourself, my precious boy, will you? There is the little medicine-case that the church gave me at the time of our silver-wedding."

"Don't mother!" pleaded Horace, choking.

"No, mother," interposed the elder, taking her hands away from the bag, "the boy can't stand it. He'll remember how everything in here has been sprinkled over with your tears, and he'll remember how much we dote on him and on his return as an honorable man. He'll put this in his pocket—it may stop a bullet," whipping out a Testament from his own pocket. "It'll shield you from Satan's darts. It's the one your old father's used in the parish nigh on to forty years. Maybe a text in it, you'll find marked, you'll be able to hitch some of my sermons on to—poor old sermons."

The man could not finish his little homily. As for Horace, he was speechless. He put the book in his pocket.

"And now good-bye; and may the God of battles keep you—all we have in this world!" The elder's eyes were glorious as his hands stretched out over his son's shoulder in his parting benediction.

"Mother—my God, father, she has fainted!"

"No," faintly gasped the lady. But the strong young arms lifted the little woman as if she were a child, and carried her all the way up to her easy-chair under the vine-clad veranda. He placed her there as softly as she had placed him in his cradle years ago.

"Good-bye, my darling, go," she faintly commanded; "God will be with us and you."

He bent down to her, and kissed her over and over again. Then he bounded away. Indeed, it was time. He came springing down the path, I remember. I whipped up, and off we drove as rapidly as we could. Mary told me afterwards how, as the sun went down, and the gloaming fell over all, the old preacher went up and stood by the chamber door where his son had slept from boyhood until manhood, and prayed and sobbed and committed him to God. Well he might, could he have foreseen the peril of his manhood's betrayal.

CHAPTER XII

I DO not know that any eye except my own will ever read this narrative. In fact, I am a plain man, wholly without literary ambition. I am no artist. Let me jot down the marked events, in the order of the time, just as they came.

It was at Deacon Littlefield's husking. It was on my own barn floor, but I was not master of ceremonies. During the summer, after Horace went off to the wars, Littlefield had ventured to act on the decision of the judge of probate, or surrogate, and had actually taken possession of my farm in his adopted daughter's name. Not that she had moved into the dwelling. But somebody must take care of the crops and stock, of course, and this the sharp deacon had proceeded at once to do. He had invited his neighbors to a husking-bee. I went over. All this interval I had not been idle. But on dear Mrs. Parkridge's account, and by her mysterious assurances that my time would surely come, the crisis when she could and would help me to justice, I had kept silent. I had worked hard carrying on the elder's farm, and so really supporting the family. Hor-

ace also sent his wages home, and that helped his
father out to a degree.

We were gathered on my great barn floor that
autumn evening. You may be sure my heart
was fuller than the bursting barns, but I was silent and retired. I got over near Peleg Rumney,
my hired man of former days. We both passed
the time of day pleasantly, and bent down to the
shocks between our knees. As we stripped the
ears, I suddenly demanded of the old man :

" Peleg, where is Mrs. Cark ?"

" I vum ter Moses, Mr. Stone, I dunno," was his
reply. "Ask him," with a nod of the head, indicating Mr. Littlewood on the other side of the
barn floor, where he sat husking at a shock of
corn, as busy as any of his guests.

"Peleg," I insisted, in a low tone behind my
shock, "I have waited all summer patiently.
You know how ill the elder and his wife have
been. I couldn't do anything but watch and wait
on them. I haven't for months crossed the highway to come to this dwelling. Come now, old
man, I always treated you well. There is going
to be a sharp fight right off about my property.
Which side are you on ?"

But the skilfulest wheedling of kindly tones
and smiles did not avail. In fact, it had been so
all the sad and busy season whenever I had made
an attempt to see the fellow. Deacon Littlewood
had kept a detective's eye on Peleg night and
day. We called the agent, who occupied a room

in the Bosworth house, a spy. That was the usual countrymen's name for this Mr. Sheriff Hooker. All such proceedings but added to the heavy load of unpopularity under which the Littlewoods now staggered. Cynthia had been spirited away—ostensibly sent on a visit to Troy, New York, with Mr. Littlewood's brother. Every one said it was a mere ruse to keep her rebellious tongue still until the colonel could come home after some of the brave battles, and stay long enough to marry her, whether she would or not. In fact, I don't think any one would have attended this husking-bee of his at Bosworth's barn except that the patriotic neighbors reflected : " Well, let's go. One thing is true: Felton's fightin' fer his country and half the corn is to go to the fair."

"Brethering," the deacon announced, "an' frends, ye understan' thet I gin bush'l fer bush'l to th' Sanitary Fair."

This patriotic promise, which had been widely proclaimed by posters, written by the deacon's own hand, at the cross-roads, had its softening influence, and probably had secured the invitations the grudging welcome that brought together a score of farmers. When now, squat behind a bundle of corn, the host was springing to his task with the utmost exertion by way of thrifty example, the farmers heard his reiteration of benevolent intent with significant smiles, as much as to say : " Oh, we know *you*."

" You don' hear no good news f'm Cap'n Parkridge, I vum ter Moses, eh ?" whispered Peleg to
me.

" He's never been hurt thus far," I answered,
evasively.

" No ? The big cunnel, I vum, sez the boy's
a-drinkin' hard, an' th' dekin's pious sorry.
When we got them letters—yer know I'm over
ter his place a good deal o' th' time—he sez, sez
he to 's wife, ' Yer see, my dear, haow foolish
Cynthy 'd ben, sez he, ef she'd a-taken thet feller.
The cuss o' th' Almighty's on th' elder's boy; an'
sez he, my cuss 'll be on Cynthy ef she don't
come back f'm Troy an' stop givin' th' mitten
thet she's ben offerin' t' our cunnel, an' upsettin'
all our plans.' "

Then the little old man chuckled to himself to
think how much wiser he apparently was as to the
real situation than I, and fell to husking with all
his might.

" Peleg, I beg you not to spread abroad this
story of Captain Hod's drinking," and I snapped
off an ear decisively and whipped it into the basket. " It will kill his father and mother, as
surely as I hit that basket with that ear, if the
disgrace of his unhappy slip gets abroad. Heaven
knows the poor old pair suffer enough now."

" Wa'al, ain't it so ?" asked he, speaking quite
loudly.

" Hush !"

" Neow, Peleg," called Littlewood, uneasily

eyeing us, though I attempted to seem more engaged with Eliphalet Hood on my left than with
Peleg—"neow, Peleg, keep 'em all a-goin'. You'll
hev ter shin up among th' dove-cotes on th' high
beams, and toss daown more stalks."

"Yis," was the ready response, as the man
promptly ran up the ladder, and began his task
above us, merrily shouting :

"Haow's thet ? sez he—an' how's thet ? sez he,"
pitching down the bundles with a resounding
crash upon the floor. "Ez the boy sed abaout
th' doughnuts, sez he, nevertheless I've eaten
three, likewise they're very good; I'll take another
also, sez he, I vum."

When he had clambered down again at my
side, I resumed :

"Peleg, how much does the deacon pay you ?"

"Powerful lib'ral."

"Do you like him better than you did me ?"

"He's a powerful pious man, Mr. 'Lisha."

"That doesn't answer my question. Now,
Peleg," I said, balancing a bright red ear on my
finger as I spoke, "count all the kernels on this
ear, give that venerable man a year in prison
for every kernel, and it will be less than he really
deserves."

Peleg was alarmed at so much as a mention of
the word prison. I saw that in his startled look.

"Peleg, now answer me," I continued ; "if you
don't want to be implicated with him and share
his fate, has the deacon not warned you to keep

out of my sight, and out of the sight of any one
from the elder's house ?"

"But Mrs. Parkridge was over here less'n a
week ago, lookin' so pale, and tryin' ter find
Polly Cark."

"Yes ; where is Polly Cark ?"

"I dunno, I vum, sez I."

"You do," I said savagely. "Tell me, or I'll
pitch you now on to the horns of the cattle !"
The little old fellow had probably never seen me
so desperately in earnest. His lower lip dropped
and he shrank away in among the corn-stalks,
putting up his crooked hands by way of defence.
I followed up my advantage, and circumstances
favored me. Mr. Littlewood had gotten the attention of the rest of the company diverted to
a husking contest. The yellow ears were flashing through the air from three huskers on a side.
The strife was to see which trio would first fill
either of the two baskets at which they shot their
husked ears. Laughter and shout resounded.
Littlewood was urging them on with the keenest
relish of a thrifty master of ceremonies. He saw
work rapidly being turned off by this means, and
fairly dancing up and down in front of them, he
shouted them to the contest. At this rate the
big barn would be well cleared by ten o'clock.

I pushed Peleg further into concealment. I
had two firm hands on his shoulders.

"Peleg, why do you suppose I consented to
come over here to work on crops that that re-

spectable thief has stolen from my acres as he
has the acres themselves ? Boy, do you not see
that we are not even on speaking terms ? I have
come here because I have got down to hard work
now with my lawyer. We are ready for battle.
I must have your help. I can't find Mrs. Cark.
She seems to have disappeared for months from
the neighborhood. I want her. You know where
she is. Tell me, or I will do with you, as a Bible
king did with Daniel, you old ingrate — I'll toss
you over in with the Durham bull in ten seconds !"

"Mis' Cark, she was driv outen house an' home
by th' ghost !"

" What ?"

" The ghost what hants th' ol' house !"

" Ghost, poor fool ? There is no such thing
on God's green earth."

"Yis, th' is. No feller can't stan' it but Mr.
Hooker, an' he sleeps with pistols. I sleep in th'
carriage-house when I stay here at all."

" Quick !"—I pursued him. " Have it so then,
but where is Cark gone ?"

"I vum ter hellylooya, ez sure's I'm passin'
through the valley 'f Jehosaphat, ez sure's I ever
sailed roun' Cape Horn an' hed th' fever 'n th'
diggin's, I dunno. She's a goner !"

I held him a moment, gazing hard at him to
make sure that he was telling the truth. I didn't
become convinced of his sincerity as against my
suspicions.

"Peleg, that woman is in the mansion. If she

is not, the ghost has flown away with her, and it
will fly away with you yet if you don't turn an
honest man. In other words, Littlewood has
sent her off to get rid of her if she is not in that
dwelling, and he will get rid of you if you do
not quit him. He will trump up some charge.
He'll get hold of some of your California scrapes."

"I vum, d'yer spose he ever heerd 'f thet man
in th' Isthmus?" The little bent fellow was
suddenly turned into a coil of springing wire.
All his senile drivellings left him. In one shud-
der he squirmed out of my grasp, and stood
erect in quite a manly fit of anger, his eyes glowing like coals in the dim light that fell from the
three swinging lanterns. I had never seen the
tiger in the man but once before. That was
several years gone by, when he brought me one
day a newspaper advertisement which was the
description of himself, accompanied with an offered reward. Then he told me his story. There
had been an adventure on the Isthmus, when a
weary party of beggarly miners were marching
from sea to sea, before the days of the railroad.
He confessed enough to make me sure that in a
desperate moment he had done a desperate deed.
All the evil in the man's nature was aroused that
day. I remember it was with difficulty I calmed
him. It had seemed to me, upon reflection at
the time, to be a merciful and proper deed to
shield a penitent old wreck of a life which was
trying to conduct itself decently at its close. I

had never referred to the subject from that day to this, but it was now my hold upon him.

"Ef I thought he was deep 'nuff fer thet"—the man slipped a knife from a curious sheath in his boot-leg, and held it aloft.

"Fool, no! Let's rather put him in prison, where he belongs. You don't want to put yourself there. Peleg, to-night you must go over the house with me and find Cark. She is there."

"When shall we start?" He sprang out eagerly.

"After the cider and apples and singing and fiddling and jigs begin," I answered. With that I released him and took my place with the circle of workmen.

"Hurrah! Northbrook forever!" burst at that instant in a rattling shout from twenty throats. It indicated that the husking contest had resulted in victory for three farmers on our road.

"Peleg! Dan-net, where is the little raskil? More stalks!" shouted Mr. Littlewood, as he pawed away the breastwork of stalks behind which we were temporarily hid. The charcoal eyes, the shaven face, the round-shouldered figure appeared to us. He was ready with a mouthful of scolding, but the moment he caught sight of Peleg, the knife still gleaming in his hand, Littlewood whipped off his frown, and masked himself with that charming smile which he always had at convenience. Most singular, most pious, most shrewd man! Never was another

12

combination of angel and devil in one person as
in him, and so perfectly self-possessed !

"Ah, boy," he said, addressing Peleg in tones
of kindly alarm, "did he attack you ?" with a nod
of his head towards me. "He's harmless, though
he'd orter be in th' 'sylum. May break out any
moment."

"No, sir, yer ol' hypercrit, I vum; it's yeou I
meant it fer."

"Me !" Littlewood started back. Then he bethought himself, wily as a cat, of the softening
influences of the feasting, perhaps remembering
Peleg's weakness for such things, for he cried
out:

"Peleg, it's time fer the cider. Go get the
cider and the pies. Ten mince-pies, and ten pun-
kin-pies, a pan o' doughnuts, and the cheese curd.
Wa'al, they're all over ter th' house."

"Littlewood," I said, "who made your pies in
that empty house ?"

"Why, dan-net—" At that moment the cattle
burst forth in one of their bellowing choruses.
This time the bleating, the bellowing, the rattling
of shining horns tipped with brass buttons clash-
ing against one another and striking against the
stanchions, the bovine alarm and protest against
such midnight intrusion by human revellers, was
more pronounced than it had been at all. Any
one who ever attended a husking-bee will recall
these occasional uproars made by cattle. A busy
millionaire railway president once said to me :

"When I am wholly worn out in the office, I sometimes close my eyes and go back again to hear the music of forty head of cattle bellowing to the light of a late lantern, swinging at my boyish hand, in front of a stanchion on a barn floor."

The noise was an excuse for Littlewood and me to break off our encounter that promised no good to either of us. The noise let Peleg slip out, scampering away to fetch the refreshment. It was an accompaniment for the cleaning up the floor with brooms. At all events, enough work had been done to match the late hour, and men were ready to eat and drink and be jolly.

"It's 'leven o'clock, neighbors an' brethering," shouted Littlewood. "You've done well—fer the fair. Neow, let's hev some new cider with no drunk in 't, and nice pies. They're a-comin'."

At that moment the last bullock at the far end of the stables sighed out his regrets, perhaps, that he and his did not eat pies. Just then, too, tripped into the centre of the group of cross-legged huskers, as they sat around the floor—who?

"Cynthia Littlewood!" Everybody exclaimed it.

"Good-evening, neighbors," she saluted us.

There was a thrill of genuine pleasure which stirred us all with that laughing salutation. She was never more beautiful, though I thought pale and thin, as I saw her under the lantern's light. She was dressed like the milkmaids in the plays

that I have seen since—white apron, pretty bare
hands carrying the plates, her dark hair adorned
with some autumn spray, I think a bit of golden-
rod, and all about her graceful self a witchery
that no man could resist without the clapping of
hands and cheers. She had such a welcome as
only honest hearts can give a lovely woman.

"She ain't party to 't," I overheard an old
farmer whisper to his neighbor.

"No; she wants ter undo 't all, and jilt th'
cunnel, and gin up the lawsuit."

This rumor of Cynthia's changed disposition
had got abroad, and was perhaps something of a
factor in the partial toleration of the Littlewood
family in the neighborhood of late.

"Wa'al, wa'al," exclaimed several voices, "and
the other beauty too!"

True enough, Mary Holyoke walked in just behind Cynthia, carrying a basketful of tumblers,
and evidently the girls were in friendly accord. I
saw immediately that Deacon Littlewood was
taken very much by surprise. The two pretty
dears had met since the morning, and had come to
know each other's minds, that I saw, and it set me
to thinking upon my problems so hard that I forgot to rise and greet the young lady, who had
just returned from her visit at Troy. But she did
not forget me, and coming over to me, she exclaimed, "We miss the boys, don't we, Elisha?"
as she handed me my plate. "Times are sad indeed. Look on this barnful of gray heads and

mere lads. No merry dancing to-night," and she tried to laugh for cheer.

"You'll see the men dance, my pretty," laughed out old Ichabod Hobbs, who sat near me and overheard her. "Wait till they've had a nip of your father's new cider."

When Mary rustled along near me I asked, eagerly, "What's in the wind now? what have you two witches been up to since I left the house?"

"Oh, the strangest of all strange things. Cynthia rode over this afternoon, to our infinite surprise, and invited me to help her here to-night, as the guests were to be all men. That was the excuse. Then we had such a long talk together, all about the sad news from Horace, and she actually cried over him. She is in love with him. She doesn't wear Felton's ring," with a shake of her pretty finger at me. "She expects him home, though, on a furlough any time, and at almost any moment. I am afraid there is to be *such* a scene then. She declares she will never keep her engagement with him, that she has practically broken it now. The best of all, she is fully in sympathy with us in securing your rights. She has discovered that she is not Mr. Bosworth's child."

"What!" But before I could snatch another word with Mary, Mr. Littlewood himself pushed in between us with some empty compliment to the young lady, and it was quite an interval before I could again get Mary's ear. Was it possible that a righteous Providence was bringing me this girl, Cynthia, at last for an ally? I picked away at my food in silence, reviewing what my lawyer had sketched out for me. The next opportunity that I could secure I said to Mary:

"Did Cynthia talk with Mrs. Parkridge?"

"Yes, she told her that we must now find Mrs. Cark; that that was the next step."

"Exactly. Did poor Mrs. Parkridge—did you —were you present while they conversed?" I asked, quite losing my self-possession in the excitement of a sudden culmination to many long-formed plans by Ashael Keep and myself.

"Yes; and poor sick woman, she was very much overcome by the fact that Cynthia had voluntarily visited us. She said that her end was nigh. She had carried some secret as long as she could, that Horace's present wrong-going was breaking her heart quite, and she had no desire to live longer. She kissed Cynthia, and asked her forgiveness—I don't quite know for what, neither did Cynthia—and she made Cynthia pledge herself to write Horace. The poor girl eagerly gave the promise, asking if Horace would indeed be glad to hear from her. Mrs. Parkridge directed her to begin her letter by saying 'in obedience to a promise made to your dying mother.'" By this time the fiddle was tuning, and the men were thumping the floor with their cowhide boots, and becoming decidedly jovial.

"What then, Mary? I cannot let you go," I cried, "till you answer me. Tell me before you and Cynthia leave." I held her by the long white string of her apron.

"I don't know just what else was said, for they two wished to be alone. When Cynthia came out into the kitchen after some minutes she was nearly hysterical. She only said, ' Where *do* you suppose Papa Littlewood—Mr. Littlewood, rather—stamping her foot, has sent Mrs. Cark ?' "

"That is what I will find out before I sleep!" I exclaimed. "Peleg shall help me—Peleg *must* be true to me," I vowed, with a blow upon my knee, as the girl sped away from me, flinging her " Heaven prosper you !" after her retreating form.

The uproarious jig of these farmers I think I witnessed, but I was not amused by it. For the first time in my life I sat apart from the jollifications of my hearty neighbors; I kept my position there, upon the floor, amid the husks. I was continually thinking, "I must have Peleg." The little old man was not to be seen. I waited for him, watched for him. I would soon go to search for him if he did not reappear; but he was still not to be seen, and Mr. Littlewood was missing also.

CHAPTER XIII

STEPPING out into the night, I encountered Littlewood talking with his factotum, Hooker, of whom I have made mention, giving the name that he was known by among the farmers—the spy.

"Where's Peleg?" demanded Littlewood. "I'm goin' hum. Cynthia must go with me. Where is the gal? The mansion seems to be shet up. I allus retire when th' hilarity begins. It's very worldly. Strange, strange that men kin git so jolly on nothin'. That there cider is only a month old."

"You must allow something for custom and great animal spirits and good cheer," responded Hooker, in his cold dry way. "It's only the good spirits of good fellers who think they've done a good deed to the fair for the soldiers, and they are having a shout at the end."

"Yis, yis. By-the-way," replied the deacon, bustling into the carriage-house and returning with a bushel-basket in his hand, "I brought this over. If they get to wantin' to measure up the corn fer the fair, use this; it's stronger."

"And smaller," chuckled Hooker, with a poke in his employer's ribs.

"Nothin' of the sort," was Littlewood's unabashed reply. "It's th' sacred bushel I allus use in dealin' with the Lord's cause. I give Him a tenth of all my income, 'n' am glad ter git off so cheap. Now, let Peleg shet up th' buildin's when they're through. Ah! here he is with the hoss. Where's Cynthy?"

"She went over to the elder's for the night," answered Hooker.

"It mustn't be!" exclaimed Littlewood, excitedly; "I'll drive over 'n' git her t' oncet. Goodnight," and he was about to whip up his animal. His solicitude about Cynthia's unexpected visit made him quite forgetful of any possible warning that he wished to leave with Peleg about having further conversation with me. Perhaps, indeed, he did not see me, as I stood under cover of the toolhouse shed.

"Mr. Littlewood," the man Hooker spoke very decidedly; so sharply, indeed, that the farmer pulled up his horse instantly.

"Well, what's wrong?"

"I sha'n't stay in that mansion another night!"

"Whew!" whispered the deacon, dropping the lines across the dashboard. "Come up ter the waggin."

Hooker obeyed, saying: "I'm good for any number of flesh-and-blood thieves, Littlewood, but spirits from another world is more'n I bargained to keep guard against."

"Cracky! But you ain't seen no angels," laughed Littlewood.

"Angel or devil, I've seen and heard enough in the two months I've occupied that house. I'm all worn out. When a feller can't sleep at night, what's life worth? So pay me to-night, and let me ride down to the four corners with you. I'll walk the rest of the way to the train at West Village."

"Oh, pooh, pooh; not ter-night," protested the deacon, evidently in the greatest perplexity.

"Yes, siree, to-night! Sit along. I've got my bag. Last night was enough for me."

"Why, man, man, I know what 'tis. 'Tain't nothin'," urged Littlewood, fairly whining out his pleading protest.

"I don't care what 'tis. Sit along! Let Peleg keep guard from his room in the stables. If the old Californian were asked to sleep in that library where I have slept of late, he'd lose all the hair that's left on his old bald pate before two nights were passed. Sit along!" And Hooker at once with no more ado climbed over the front wheel, giving his travelling-bag a sling into the back of the buggy.

Littlewood sat in blank dismay. He managed to say,

"But—but—dan-net, the gal, my darter."

"Let her spend the night with the preacher's folks. She is there already. Drive out of here before that old moon gets mooning any higher on the old pile," responded Hooker, with a thoroughly frightened glance over his left shoulder.

When a brave man once gives way to his fears
his courage melts as fast as a snowbank in June.
Hooker's blood had all turned to water evidently.
I confess to a certain contagion of his terror as I
witnessed it, it was so abject. Yet I was so
thankful for the unexpected Providence of a
clear coast, and escape from the need of playing
burglar, that I could scarce refrain my lips from
crying out my gratitude.

"Well," meditated Mr. Littlewood, in ugly de-
cisiveness, "nothin' frightens me—except my
woman's tongue," with a chuckle. "If 't warn't
fer her, I'd stay myself, 'n' let Cynthy sleep at
th' elder's. Old Lady Parkridge's pooty sick,
but she'll not say nothin' yit. Peleg!" he
shouted at length, and as the little old man
obediently dodged from the stable into a broad
bar of moonlight his employer gave his orders:
"Hooker's sick, orful sick, got ter take him t' th'
doctor's ; yer look arter things all raound till I
come over 'n the mornin', or perhaps sooner.
G' lang, Dob," and with a slap of the thin black
lines across the horse's hips away the pair rattled
out over the shining gravelled driveway. I remember that distinctly—do I not?—that he remarked, "Old Mrs. Parkridge 'll say nothing
yet."

For myself, I climbed up on the seat of a mow-
ing-machine in the black shade of the tool-house
shelter. The flood of silver from the moon, just
on a level with the horizon, lay like a glistening

carpet along the frosty earth. I sat there, thinking, till the last farmer had at length come out from the husking hilarities, and had gone with his chattering fellows various ways over field and highway. Peleg at length began to shut his doors. I heard them bang and bang one after another. Then, as the old miner issued forth from the barnyard gate, I slipped down and suddenly confronted him.

"All ready, my brave fellow?"

"Master Stone, what is it?" he cried, with a look of pretended surprise.

"All ready to go upon our search for Mrs. Cark—Polly, our excellent Polly—who must have left some line, some farewell message of direction for her few friends, as she departed to regions unknown. We must look for her, old boy, or for a line in reference to her, in yonder," pointing towards the residence.

"I won't!" He spoke decisively enough, but I could see that he was fairly white with fear.

"Oh, yes, you will. Go get the extra key that is doubtless hanging in the harness-room. Come, be quick, man; this is not as hard a night's work by any means as you have undertaken in the course of your somewhat checkered career."

I threw him one significant glance, and then let him off upon his errand. He went, oh yes. He obeyed. He had better! He was gone a long time. I kept my station in the solemn, deserted yard in the rear of the mansion. The effect of the great golden harvest moon, as yet so low down that its huge sickle seemed to threaten the gable of neighbor Kipling's hill-top barn, was to fill the broken country with stalking shadows everywhere, and shadowy things seemed to be creeping away from me as the light mounted higher. The cone-shaped shadows of the firs by the garden wall, the cobweb of my windmill, which at first lay about my feet in a tangle, and the menacing finger of the stumpy spire on the carriage-house among the trees slipped away—all of these slipped away from me farther and farther, and left me standing in the light.

"Like my unhappy days and troubles," I meditated, speaking aloud to the night.

The wide brick dwelling burst slowly into grace and glory in glaring contrast with its aspect of neglect by peeling dingy paint, as seen of late in the glare of day.

"Perhaps, at last, after all this laying of plans, light is coming on my way," I said, still talking to the night.

I fell into such a reverie that I forgot my man. Moving around a little to the left, I studied the tall, dark windows, each one of which seemed sealed so closely that I found it hard to believe a living human being was hiding behind any one of them. I saw again the old Senator in memory, as I can just dimly recall him, by the great front door, leaning on his stick, consulting his morning weather-gauges. I was often sent over

here on errands. Doubtless it was the tinkling
of the thin streams in the iron fountain—what a
shame to leave the water on so late in the fall!—
sounds of splash and tinkle, I say, that suddenly
seemed a voice. It resembled so startlingly the
Senator's whisper and wheeze between his coughs
and his call:

"Boy, how are the folks over to Holyoke's?
What's your errand? Let us have it, and then
go. I like boys best when a good ways off."

Then, friendless little farm-hand that I was,
not knowing what day kind Abner Holyoke
might say he had got through haying and the
tedder-boy might find another job, still I used to
stare back at the grim, stately old Senator, and
console myself with the thought,

"I'm glad he is not my father."

As now I stealthily crept around the corner of
the dwelling the silent knoll where my mother
slept came in full view, on a straight line through
the stately pillars where the Senator should have
been standing if alive. I don't know why, but
somehow I connected the two for the first time
in my life; doubtless because both had passed
on into that impenetrable mystery suggested by
the fair head-stones on the hill. The Senator's
ashes, however, did not rest yonder. That much
I knew. Where they were buried I do not think
I knew.

Still I lingered and dreamed inactive, waiting
for my man's return. I do not think in all my

days I had ever given that rich old lord of the hills so much thought as now. I could have easily imagined him watching me, fully revealed by some strange function of memory; and when I contrasted my present stature with my boyish aspect those years gone by, this most curious mental impression suddenly seized upon me, namely, I was sure that I had grown to resemble that tall, broad-shouldered gentleman. I had myself, in turn, come to man's estate, as he was when I remembered him in his prime and day of honors.

"The outrage of it is, sir"—I found myself apostrophizing the former owner, standing there—"the outrage of it is that all this was, *is*, the once friendless boy's property ; purchased, these acres, by his thrift and savings. And this mansion, once—yes—ah, I burn so, old sir, when I think of it, how I have been defrauded by some curious fatality, that I have kept myself from even crossing the highway for months lest I yield and set a torch to the pile !"

"Here is the key."

I turned, in astonishment, to confront both Mary Holyoke and Cynthia Littlewood ! They had approached me from behind, so noiselessly flitting along their way as I stood near the grass border that I had heard not even the fall of a footstep. They were clinging timidly together, and Mary at once placed her hand within my arm. The night, now breathing mists, had sprayed their faces with diamond-powder, which glistened in the soft moonlight.

"This is wrong, girls."

"It is right," answered Mary.

"Peleg has turned coward ; but he brought the key over to the elder's, if he would not bring it to you," Cynthia chimed in.

"How is the sick woman?"

"Much worse — the excitement of dear Cynthia's coming," answered Mary. "We were sitting in her chamber. I suppose Peleg saw the light, and brought us there the key and his lantern."

"Not only my coming, I fear, has affected poor dear Mrs. Parkridge," Cynthia explained, clutching closer Mary's arm as Mary clung closer by the second to me, "but that again there is no Thursday's letter from Horace, so she says. Three weeks now—what can have happened? And all the more strange, because the regiment is certainly in New York city to quell some rioting if it should occur. I know this, because I am any moment expecting to see Colonel Felton here, running up from New York. He wrote me to that effect."

I made them no reply regarding Horace. My own heart was too full of forebodings, and of the probable explanation of his silence, but I asked, abruptly :

"Do you really wish to enter on this search with me, and probably meet Mrs. Cark, at this hour of the night?"

"Certainly," responded Mary; "Mrs. Parkridge herself has directed us to do so."

"And my lawyer, Keep, urges that there must be no further delay."

"And especially now that I inform you of Colonel Felton's probable reappearance at any instant," added Cynthia.

"Come on!" I promptly replied.

We crossed the yard to the broad flight of shallow stone steps. An owl remonstrated from some lawn tree to the northward. A bat darted out to greet us with a sinister circle, leaving her concealment under the stone cornice above the great door. A gust of wind from the north hills —the first stir of air in all this still night thus far —gently folded a mass of river fog about us, obscuring the moon in its ghastly veil. But we pushed straight on now, and the next moment entered the house.

"What a clang to that great door! how it echoes!" Suddenly Cynthia spoke it, while I paused in the heavy air of the hallway to strike the lantern light. "What is that?" she exclaimed, as two sharp strokes of an alarm-bell saluted her ears.

"Why, it's Elisha's own clock on the stair," answered Mary.

"Two o'clock at night, November 28, 18—. Hooker has kept the venerable timepiece faithfully wound, has he not? Please God, the old clock shall mark many a happy hour here yet for

13

us and ours and all our friends," I answered, my spirits rising as theirs seemed to fall.

Crossing the great hall we began to ascend the stairs, when Cynthia turned back to survey in the dim light the confusion of the littered apartments. Rolls of new carpeting, boxes of furniture, and several ungainly shapes of sacking, which seemed almost human and ready behind us to start trooping after up the winding stair.

"All this reminds you of a narrow escape from an unhappy—what would surely have been an exceedingly unhappy life?" asked Mary.

"If I only *were* escaped!" was the dark girl's reply, and with that she darted on before us. At the head of the stair she stopped short, turned to the right, uttered a little shriek, which ended in a low, trembling wail. The echo of that voice thrilled me, and my nerves are pretty steady, too.

Mary stopped and clutched my arm vigorously; then gasped, "What is it?" But instantly, like the reasonable woman she is, she recovered her good common-sense, and flung my arm away from her as she flew up to the landing, and bent to lift the half-fainting Cynthia, who was pointing towards the left wing of the building.

A peculiar light fell and fluttered over her, with alternation of shadow and glow, somewhat like the effects that I have since seen produced in tableaux. A man's stride is slower than a woman's flight, and I had full opportunity to witness this as I was stumbling upward towards the girls.

Once by their side, I saw at the farther end of
the hall what I expected—the wrinkled witch, the
object of my long search—the wished-for sight of
a person whom Keep and I had considered necessary for our suit during many a day.

"Mrs. Cark! Polly, you poor deceiver!" I
cried, " the jugglery of your lamp and your grotesque dress cannot deceive us. You certainly
have succeeded in making yourself look frightful,
but we recognize you. What is your purpose?"

I addressed her at such length as to give her
small opportunity to play any of her graveyard
tricks upon us. She listened; she lowered the
lamp, a curious flambeau that her own ingenuity
had produced, and her eyes paused on me move-
less till I ceased.

"I have had a long imprisonment," she sighed.
" I am not sorry to see you, though I bear no love
for you, Elisha Stone, nor for Mary Holyoke."

"What have you to say of me?" asked Cynthia, pleadingly.

CHAPTER XIV

THE haggard masquerader regarded Cynthia Littlewood a moment with a fixed stare, a stare which softened and hardened by turns. There were for a moment the tenderest emotions struggling in the features of the unhappy woman, then, as over the valleys amid the mountains a cloudy day brings forbidding gloom, a darker look filled her countenance and forbade all loving approach.

"I would walk around the world to save your feet, Cynthia, a single step too many." She spoke very abruptly. "But nothing seems to save you. You will not save yourself." She ceased speaking without approaching us.

Remember that I knew nothing of what Mother Parkridge had been saying to Cynthia.

"Do you say so?" answered Cynthia, offering to draw near her. I was astonished by the girl's tones of tenderness. "Let me come and kiss you, poor lady. What does all this shutting up here mean? How dreadful all this ghostly business is in our quiet neighborhood. Why are you here? What do you know about me?"

She rained such questions as these upon Cark, .

one after another, until poor Polly seemed to be dazed by them and by their eagerness.

"Stop! Don't come near me, Cynthia!" she protested. "I couldn't go on with my part if I were once to hold you in my arms."

"There is no reason under heaven, woman, why you should stay here and play the lunatic," I put in. "Why have you kept yourself hidden away from our sight?"

"Ask Deacon Littlewood," she answered.

"What has he to do with you?" I demanded, as I alone made bold to walk over to her side.

"It was a choice between this—and the asylum or prison," she answered.

"Explain further," I said.

"In an unfortunate moment of great joy, as I then thought, and such a moment is rare to me, when I learned that his daughter Cynthia was to be married, in order that I might keep my old place and be near—I would say, continue to earn my bread—I allowed myself to say something to Mr. Littlewood and Mr. Felton one day that I ought never to have said." Then she paused so long that I must needs prompt her.

"Well, why ought you not to have said it, and do you mind telling us what it was that you should not have said?" I asked.

"I ought not to have said it, Elisha Stone, because when one begins with a falsehood in early life, after a time the lie becomes a devil, a very demon, a monster from hell, and one must needs die standing by her lie, or the truth, if spoken, will take some one's life whom you hold dear."

" Whose life?"

" Mrs. Parkridge's, for one."

" You are mistaken now, Polly," I said; " for she, too, has been seeking you in vain, and urged us most pathetically to find you and hear something that you had to say. Tell her," with a motion of my head towards Cynthia, " whose child she is."

" I knew Cynthia's mother."

" Oh, tell me of her," pleaded the girl, sweeping forward and falling on her knees as she caught the retreating woman and held her fast. " When some years ago I first knew it, I felt it, that Mrs. Littlewood was not my own mother, the lonely thought began to distress me so! Whose child am I? I have known of late that Mr. and Mrs. Littlewood have been using me to further their own fortunes. And I am not Mr. Bosworth's child, am I? "

" Woman !" I suddenly cried, addressing Polly, " be careful of that torch ; it is leaking fire on the girl's dress."

She righted her camphene torch for a moment, while I sprang to the left and scuffled my heavy boots over the flaming spots that darted a dozen tiny tongues up at me from the floor. The interruption and fright were profitable for our greater familiarity, and we fell after it into a more natural posture all around, as became flesh-and-blood beings in a natural world.

"I knew your mother, too." Mrs. Cark addressed me now.

"No doubt of it, Polly. But first as to Cynthia."

Again the gaze of tenderness was bent on the beautiful young woman who had sunk once more at her feet. It was a loving look for a moment; but then, as if by some powerful resolution, or suddenly stung to its death by an ugly memory, the softened look changed into a hard, unfeeling stare as before, and she answered me:

"Does Mrs. Parkridge consent that I may reply to your questions?"

"Yes, yes," interrupted Mary, coming forward and putting a caressing hand on the woman's shoulder; "she says it is time to do right, time that we all began to act sensibly. Here is Elisha defrauded of his property by unwilling Cynthia."

"Unwilling?" shaking off Mary's touch.

"Certainly she does not wish to marry Felton, nor to possess this property. It is by his prompting."

"And I will not, oh, I will not marry him!" cried Cynthia, springing to her feet and daring to throw herself on Polly's breast.

The clear ringing tones of the girls could undoubtedly have been distinctly understood in the lower hall of the building. The echo of their stout protest was yet sounding and enforcing its silence on us all when we heard a masculine voice ascending the stairs.

"That's her lie to me!" It was Arthur Alfred Felton's voice which came up through the darkness. Immediately after it came this other voice, saying :

"Darter, darter, Heaven 'll smite th' disobedient!"

Mrs. Cark lifted her sputtering torch with a snatch and jerk into the air. I held aloft my lantern. Colonel Felton and Mr. Littlewood were promptly revealed on the upper landing. Without waiting their nearer approach I asked Littlewood :

"How much did you pay Hooker and Peleg for the treason that gave you this information?"

"Never mind—I diskivered yer. Yer liable— yer liable fer breakin' 'n' enterin'. Neow, Polly, we want yer. Come, git yer traps. Yer ain't told nothin', I hope? Remember, th' All-Seein' Eye 's on yer."

He came directly on, as if to seize her. I offered to step between them.

"Stand aside!" the wild woman hissed like a fury. "I need no defender against that man!"

"For Heaven's sake, be careful of that torch!" I expostulated ; for she swung it like a dreadful weapon, and the dropping little tongues of flame streaked the darkness, imperilling us all.

"Let Stone take it, Polly," said Littlewood, persuasively, using that smile of which I have made mention, as he started back a step for fear of some spatterings of fire.

"I have other use for it," she answered, gathering the staff of her torch in both her hands.

Again I busied myself with extinguishing the flaming drops upon the floor, at the same time reassuring by a whispered word the frightened girls who stood clinging to each other behind me.

"Let's be reasonable, my dear madame," exclaimed Colonel Felton.

"Stop!" she cried. "Cynthia, step here—face him! Do you wish to marry this man?"

Gliding to Mrs. Cark's side, and yet half-shielding herself behind the woman, the girl was about to answer, when Felton, with an oath, sprang at her with every sign of personal assault; but before he could advance I stood on the intervening boards of that floor promptly enough, you may be sure.

"Cynthia Littlewood," he shouted, "unless you keep your faith with me, I suppose you wish to engage yourself to that grand specimen of a man, Major Horace Parkridge, cashiered officer, disgraced outcast, wandering about the saloons of New York City;" and he laughed derisively.

"O God, it cannot be so!" moaned Cynthia, clasping her hands, as I have seen a marble statue in a cathedral over a tomb, and her cheeks were as bloodless as that marble.

"Don't believe it!" cried Mary Holyoke, springing to her side. "Oh, don't believe it, my dear! Even if it were so, God is great and good, and can save to the uttermost."

"Speak, my girl!" demanded Mrs. Cark, in shrill tones; "here in my presence give him his reply."

"I have written you, Colonel Felton," resumed Cynthia, raising her great eyes to gaze fully upon him, and speaking with most impressive dignity. "I wrote you that I believed you were an adventurer; that I had ceased to love you, if indeed I ever did; that I prayed God to forgive me for my wrong to Horace Parkridge, and the mischief that my coquetry had wrought. Beyond that, it is none of your business to know what my heart may prompt me to do with regard to the dear boy. But, sir"—and she grew more beautiful by her high resolve each instant—"I here charge you with his ruin. You, *you* put the cup to his lips anew. You knew the sad story of his frailty in the past, and availed yourself of it for his eternal destruction, if possible. You, who could not destroy him in battle, nor give him a position where courage would win him anything but added honor, you tempted him. I say in the presence of these all, what you boasted to me in your letters which came in reply to my own, like a cruel taunt. You said, 'Take him, then; I have succeeded in getting his old habit grafted on the lovelorn wretch once more!'" Then, turning to Deacon Littlewood, the brave girl went on: "Oh, sir, to think I ever should have to bring my lips to charge it on the man who fed them in their infancy! But I have many other things to say to you at another time—this is enough now. As a professor of the religion which you have taught in the church where you are an officer, how can you longer co-operate with this man Felton in the great wrong he is doing to others in this community?"

"My dear child, I can't 'low yer t' lose all these fine acres," the old man began to protest.

"I am not your child, nor Senator Bosworth's child."

Mr. Littlewood gasped, stammered, coughed, and looked around, but made no reply. In fact, Felton gave him short opportunity to reply, for with an added curse, which I will not record, turning to me savagely, he said:

"So, you cowardly stay-at-home, you have been working out all this while your betters have been engaged in nobler things; but you will fail, Littlewood," flinging the explanation over his shoulder towards him without looking at him, and all the while blazing at me, his hands clinched, his feet bringing him by the inch nearer and nearer with every word, "We have fixed that. She signed the marriage deed."

"Oh, I never did — never, never!" protested Cynthia, stepping forward almost to meet him. "You prepared a legal paper. You said, 'When we are man and wife, may I be master of the Bosworth place, as you will have the Littlewoods' property in your own right?' I replied, 'Yes; when we own it, and also when we are actually wed.' 'True,' you assented, 'but see how easily I could put your name in here.' "

The literal and circumstantial details of this history seemed to put even Colonel Felton's assurance out of countenance, and for a moment he was silent, which gave me my opportunity to say: "Forger, you have since done it! You have put her name in there, if you have any such paper."

"Look for yourselves," he cried, instantly producing the deed and quickly pulling it open, while he pointed to Cynthia's name in the proper blank.

"U-h-m," groaned Deacon Littlewood, exultingly—that peculiar groan which I have tried before to describe, and presume no language can depict. "How is that?"

We were now drawn into a knot of heads, except the two white heads, Polly's and Deacon Littlewood's, to study the instrument in question and examine it critically. I held the lantern high above them all. Felton kept the paper in his clutch meanwhile. The signature was so accurate that Mary and I were dismayed. As we all started away from the fateful paper, I said to Cynthia :

"That signature, if genuine, makes you a criminal, poor girl."

"But it is not genuine," she answered, not offended by my words, lofty and immovable in defiance of her accuser ; "and if it is not genuine, as it is not, it makes him a criminal. That is what you are," with a menace of her graceful forefinger at him.

" Certainly," was my quiet comment.

The words had scarcely left my lips when the man slipped a revolver from his breast. I knew not which of us he menaced, nor did I wait to discover. I hope he meant me. Let it be so put on paper. The most dastardly deed of a coward we will not write against him. He would not have shot a woman, young, lovely, and once nearly his bride. I happened to be holding the huge door-key in my hand, such a door-key as the locksmiths of a former generation wrought to move the great bolts of heavy oaken portals. It was like a hammer. I threw it with the aim that only a farmer's boy ever acquires. It struck Felton's hand. It was done as quick as a flash. The revolver fell and exploded as it struck the floor. No one was harmed. I was on him in a moment, and bore him down with a fall that shook the building.

It was just then, in her wild misery, that Polly Cark whirled her camphene torch, like a veritable Witch of Endor, and flung it—God only knows why, but obedient to some wretched impulse—crashing and spurting inextinguishable flame through the doorway of that room in the L. It was her room, her grotesque den, filled with combustible trinkets, hung with tattered lace curtains and gewgaws that were food for a conflagration.

" Fire ! fire !   Why, dan-net to dannation, th'
hag's set th' old pile on fire !" yelled Mr. Littlewood, as he turned his back on us and began
scampering **towards** the **stairway** with all his
might.

CHAPTER XV

A BURNING farm-house is the most helpless thing on earth. It is left to burn. Who shall help it, poor thing? Not the trees which fling their shrivelling arms and lash themselves in such a passion of pity, as they resolve at length to die with the roof that they have so long shaded. Not the robber winds that suddenly spring out of the valleys, massing from the four quarters of heaven at once in the stillest landscape, whistling to each other, these mischief-loving winds, as they congregate, "Lo, here is sport!" and then snatching the crumbling shingles piecemeal, and bearing them aloft with many a whirl towards the defenceless out-houses, stables, and haystacks.

Help, oh, help! But who can? What can? Not the late flocking wild-geese journeying southward that night to escape the winter's cold, who fell into the fierce heat, with the purple doves from their cot in the northwest tower. It was terrible when we had escaped and stood watching what no human hand could defend, as it crumbled in the hot flame and fell into its own red throat. Nor could the bellowing cattle help the unhappy dwelling, nor the bleating sheep, nor the horses that struck their hoofs in protest, neighing from the stables, " Help, help !"

The farmers came tramping through the fields, and one by one threw their legs over the fences, each armed with his useless pail. The gables of the neighboring farm-houses for four or five miles away blushed in the red light, and the window-sashes gleamed as if in their own conflagration. There were no engines, no bells to call to neighbors, only the faint, far-going cry of neighbor after neighbor, as each, aroused from his slumbers, sprang across his threshold and cried to the black night :

" Fire ! fire ! fire !" As if we did not all know it. What is the use of calling like that, unless it be that it is a form of prayer.

We all stood there, mute, motionless. I felt the hot tears run down my cheeks. I held Mary by the hand and spoke to her hoarsely: " My darling, so go up in this mountain cloud of cinders all my dreams of this home with you. I am so glad now that I lingered long the night before when it was in its beauty calm and glowing in the moon, and made a picture forever of the old dwelling on my brain."

The man Felton sat on the garden wall, his fine features ugly with a smirk. The deacon was in his buggy out on the drive towards the gates, determined at least to save the beast and the vehicle, and apparently careless of Cynthia, who

crouched beside Mrs. Cark, about whose bony
shape she pityingly wrapped her own shawl.
We continually retreated, little by little, before
the increasing heat, till we were half-way to the
gates, when Elder Parkridge came running out to
meet us.

"I dared not leave her to come sooner," he
shouted on before him. "I fear this will be the
last straw to break her back. But, 'Lish, it's only
the L that's on fire yet. There's a brick partition between that part and the main dwellin'. If
you could save the roof from sparks—now that
this wind is from the east it will help you to live
up there."

I sprang up, crying : "Thank you ; I am a dull
and slow fellow, but I am no craven. The ladders, the ladders !" I yelled my appeal as I
leaped towards the barns.

A score of men rushed to help me. We raised
the ladder and I went first, as I ought. We
formed a line of men and women ; Mary, Cynthia,
the farmers' daughters and wives, even poor frail
Polly Cark helping to compose this line. The
elder stood at the fountain and dipped in the
pails. From hand to hand they flew, the dripping
pails. We men stood in our blue woollen stock-
ing-feet on the roof. All the boys were with me
there, except the hardiest and strongest, who
were away at the wars. It was a long fight.
The ghostly light of morning was visible in the
east at last, and, thank God and his angels, we pre-

14

vailed in the end. Breathless, yet vigilant, erect there upon the gable, I remember that I stood watching, while catching my breath, the day as it grew lighter and lighter with a sweet, pure white radiance; watching as the dull red of the dying conflagration grew fainter and fainter. At last the sun burst in his brightness over the mountains. In his beams I lifted myself up, and while they cheered faintly, that little band of my neighbors, I lifted my cap and reverently said:

"My God, I thank Thee for the favoring winds, for the kindly help of loving friends, and for strength."

The entire main edifice was intact, but smoke-grimed, cruelly injured, and most pitiable under the strong light of the sun.

"The part where th' ghost lived 's a-goner, 'n' th' ol' house 'll be th' sweeter fer 't," cried Farmer Kipling up to me from the yard. That recalled my thoughts. At length as I descended the ladder, and mingled with the group upon the grass, I missed the elder and Mary.

"They have gone to the house," explained Cynthia.

"That forged paper!" I whispered to her. "It is all-important if we are to pursue his punishment."

"Oh, oh," exclaimed Cynthia; "but, of course, it was burned."

"It fell on the floor," I ejaculated. "That was this side of the doorway," and without another word I strode off upon my search for it.

As I entered the lower hall I caught a glimpse of Felton on the stairs descending. He threw himself out quickly at the round window half-way down. He must have seen me, for the light from the open door behind me would have revealed me. Evidently he thought himself concealed by the murky, smoke-laden air that filled the mansion. Perhaps I imagined it—his laugh of exultation. He had preceded me in the search. Had he found the fatal paper, and, therefore, laughed derisively at my defeat, or had he assured himself that it was destroyed, and never could be produced against him and the deacon? I did not then know. Groping my way up the stairs, I saw at a glance the futility of all search. The entire end of the structure towards the west was open to the day, and the east wind was sweeping up from the lower hall across the floor, carrying out the smallest particles of dust into the abyss of smoke and dying embers.

"Come on, yer smart feller," Mr. Littlewood was saying, as a few moments later I stepped from the door; "yer, Colonel Felton, with all yer brass buttons on, I mean. Come on, 'n' go hum 'th me." He had turned his vehicle round and was headed towards the barns.

"Some thanks are due the men for saving our property," said Felton.

"Wa'al, neow, whose property 's this? I guess we'd better settle that question fust," growled the shrewd deacon.

Felton pondered the question a moment, bit his lip, threw me a look, half defiance, half fear, and then got in with the old man. They turned to the rear farm drive, passed the barns, and so disappeared without the need of further meeting with the groups of neighbors around the fountain.

As I approached the group of honest fellows, my kind neighbors, some one proposed three cheers, " 'N' may yer yet git yer own, fire and fraud not countin'!"

When the cheers had ceased, I said, " Friends, I'm sure I don't know how to thank you." I got so far with my speech, when, looking casually to my right, I descried Mary Holyoke running like a deer out at a distant farm gate of the Parkridge place. I paused to look at her. On, breathlessly on, she came, till at the granite posts of our entrance she paused, put her hand to her side and leaned hard by the stone for support. Others had been watching all this with me.

" Somethin' happened. Th' gal's outer breath," cried a boy.

" I'll go meet her. She's been workin' passin' pails o' water here with the rest on us," quickly echoed another.

But it was I who went to meet her, outstripping boys and men. " What is it, Mary?" I shouted, before I had reached her.

" Oh, quick!" she gasped, pressing her heart, and for the first time in her life Mary Holyoke's cheeks were colorless.

As soon as I reached her I said : "Lean on me, dear heart, and walk slowly. Never mind telling me the message. I know it is something wrong over there. We will go and see."

But she insisted on resuming her tidings between her gasps.

"Dear Mrs. Parkridge, we fear, is dying—the fire shock was enough—but—when Polly Cark—came in—that was more. Polly—fell on—the pillow, sobbing and caressing her. The worst—was —when the poor, imprudent, well-meaning Polly—moaned out—that—deplorable tale about Horace —which Felton brought us."

"Great God!" I cried to Heaven, "can you forgive that in addition to all the rest of her mischief?"

"Wait. Then Horace's mother—rose up in bed. With a face full of intense maternal distress she cried out: 'Where is Elisha Stone? Call him. He promised to—' And then she fell back insensible."

We went directly to the chamber of the invalid, whom we all loved so dearly. The moment I entered the room Mrs. Parkridge, who had revived, cried out to me in strong tones:

"Elisha Stone, you once solemnly promised to obey me. Leave all, and go seek Horace. He is in the den of lions."

"I will go," I answered, reverently, pausing at the foot of the bed. "God give you ease of mind, dear soul."

"And I want you to go with him, my husband," she directed, lifting her thin hands to clasp him about the neck as he stood beside her bed.

The tall clergyman bent lower, yielding to her caress, and kissed her; but though he did not speak any dissent to her wishes, his countenance indicated a protest. I came near, and she drew me down, giving me at once this message for Horace:

"Tell him that his mother will not die till she sees him once more. Tell him, how like the dear light of heaven is the love his mother cherishes for him. Tell him that no shame, no misstep and its anguish, no wandering from the true and right way, can ever avail against the forgiving grace of God and a mother's love. As his father will be with you, he will say what only a priest of Christ can say when he is a father and the sinner is his only boy. But bid him return here. Here is health of body and soul. Here is Cynthia—yes, tell him Cynthia waits, and that a mother's blessing waits to pour itself out on their two heads."

"Dear loving heart," exclaimed Cynthia, entering to hear that last. And then the dark girl gave me a message, quick as thought, to add to the mother's, as I went my way for the erring. She seemed for an instant as she opened her lips to be struggling with some maidenly reserve; but then, remembering the duty she owed them all, she said, quickly:

"Tell him to come quickly back here to the hills. It is all sorrow without him; it will be all joy with his coming. Tell him I confess my wrong, and want to right it." With that she broke away from us, hiding her blushing face behind her hands as she left the room.

"What time does the Montreal Express pass south through West Village, Abner?" asked the elder of Mr. Holyoke.

I saw that that settled it. In less than an hour we were seated in the buckboard, with Mary to drive and return the team. At the station I said to Mary,

"You will see Ashael Keep?"

"Yes, everything is left at loose ends, I know, but I will do my best. Let's see," and she whipped out her tablet and pencil, "See Keep. Watch the next move of Littlewood and Felton," and she pencilled down memoranda of conversations she had heard that eventful night.

"Try to have Cynthia remain at the elder's."

"Yes, and Mrs. Cark—shall she talk, or wait until you return?"

"That depends on the action of our enemy."

"Have we all the money we want for the journey?" asked the elder, suddenly arousing himself from the lethargy of heartache.

Mary gave me a look commanding silence. I only reassured him. In fact, I had the most of that dear girl's wages for the school-teaching of the summer in my pocket-book for this journey. She had pressed it upon me. "Take it. It is for the service of their son. Have they not given us a roof for months?" I had also the money from three tons of the elder's hay, sold at the village scales two weeks before. How strange it seems to me to-day to write down such penury and close counting of dollars in that hard time of duty, but we were wretchedly poor.

"There comes the train," cried Mary. "Telegraph the first news you hear. God speed you."

We spoke no further good-byes. As the wheels began to move I looked at my watch. It was only ten o'clock. "The smoke of my half-burned home must be about as large in volume as ever," I remarked to the elder.

"It seems all a dream, so quick, so many things since ten o'clock yesterday. O God! spare her life till we find him. Boy," addressing me directly, "when you are married, and have children, you will find a strange state of things in your heart. At first you love the woman you wed the best of all the earth. Then the children seem about as dear. As time creeps on, however, the children come and go, here and there; but the wife— oh, the wife, the companion heart, and the mate to your own life, she is the most precious—she remains. I don't know as I ought to say so either, yet—I go because I love my boy, don't I? Yes, but I go mostly because I love her, and to find him will bring her up from her bed of languishing," and he hid his face behind his hands, while his distress relieved itself apparently in prayer.

I telegraphed back at White River Junction,

asking Dr. Brown to answer us at Springfield how Mrs. Parkridge had passed the day. In the gloom of a rainy night I groped around that since familiar old station until I got my reply: "She will live until you find the boy."

As the train rattled on the elder would not try to sleep—he wished to talk—so I gave up the attempt myself, and offered what consolation a loving listener might. These are some of the things he said :

"I would like to take Hod Parkridge on my knee and spank him most to death ! Then I would bury him in my heart, dear child.

"Parents know that it is full as important that a boy's wife be a good girl as that a daughter's husband be a good man, because boys are more naturally wild. If a husband wrecks your daughter's life, she will come home to you, and you can heal her heart; but if another woman wrecks your boy's life, where will he go, following Satan?

"What pay does a fellow get in serving Satan to compensate him for his mother's losing her pride in him?

"If Hod could suffer all alone, I would let him. I don't know but I could stand my part of it; but when I see his mother suffering, my sorrow is just doubled up, and I can't stand it. It chokes me to death, because I loved his mother when she was the fairest daughter of Eve that the sun ever shone upon.

"I believe Hod's mother loves him better than

she loves me, and I'm glad of it. She loves me as she loves herself. That is the Lord's rule, and all man can ask; but she loves him better than she loves herself, and that is divine.

"No doubt Hod would give up his life for me, but would he give up his bad habit of drink for me? It is more than life when it gets hold of a fellow. Only Christ can shake off that grip of a bad habit.

"I believe God loves poor Hod better than he does the cool scoundrel Felton, who never drinks, who says there is no God, who has never known any God but self.

"I'm sure there are lots of good angels this moment looking and watching over Hod, but I am afraid the angels have got scared off from walking around Mr. Littlewood lately. Professions ain't possessions."

When at last he slept I watched the white-haired clergyman as faithfully as he and his wife had watched the night through, according to the country custom, with my mother's lifeless form years before.

CHAPTER XVI

"Now, then, to look for a needle in a haymow," sighed Elder Parkridge, wearily, as we stepped from the cars in New York. Those were in the old days when the trains were dragged through Fourth Avenue by horses. Then the street-cars took us down to the vicinity of the City Hall.

"Suppose we look for a bite of something to eat first," I answered, reassuringly. We jostled along among the hurrying crowd of passengers, most of whom seemed going in the great city as straight as a rifle-ball to its mark.

After we had broken our fast we began that weary thing, a search. A search for a lost person is the utmost contradiction of words. You have a definite object before you, yet, in fact, you have nothing before you. You think of a single face; you are conscious of a sea of faces. Your tongue is ever ready to exclaim, "I have found you!" Your thought is ever forced to exclaim, on second look of the eyes, "I do not want you."

"Have we nothing whatever to guide us, no clew at all?" asked the elder, as we walked down Broadway.

"Yes, we will go down to a place called the

Battery. That is a city park. His regiment is in camp there. I do not believe that he has been cashiered, as Felton calls it; that is, discharged from the army."

"God forbid that! No, no, but Felton may have set such a scheme in motion."

"Then he will be under arrest there," I replied.

"But no; in that case Felton ought to be present, for Horace is a major of his regiment—brevet-major, you know," the elder explained, and I tried to review our home discussion of what brevet meant.

"But he was still in command of his company?"

"Yes, I understand so." Then we jogged on with occasional original commands from my companion, such as "One man is of no great account amid so many, 'Lish, as are crowding along these sidewalks. So would you think unless you stopped to think again that the sparrows are often as thick on an oat-field as the men and women are on these pavements, and not one of them falls without our Father. There ain't any home-feeling about such a crowd of money-getting, pushing, scrambling, flock-of-sheep-over-the-wall humanity, and they all act as if the dogs were after them. Still they're human like the rest of us; I count 'em as a whole—all men and women. I always assure myself by saying that."

He kept up this quaint moralizing to stay his fainting heart, no doubt. And as we came in sight of the custom-house, in walking down Wall Street, the elder exclaimed: "It's the same Uncle Sam, our Uncle Sam," pointing to the flag with his umbrella, which he insisted on carrying.

"Can you direct us to the Battery?" I asked of a policeman. The man could not literally look down on one of my stature, but mentally he did. I was a countryman in his eye evidently. He pointed but did not otherwise direct the way. Having turned about by the man's direction, we trudged on.

The tremendous strides of my companion attracted the attention of the people as he walked down the thoroughfare, half a pace ahead of me at my best, his black satchel a swinging balance in his left hand. People smiled, I observed, until they noticed his noble head; the fine features, the shapely brow with its fringe of white hair, and the pathos in his tender eyes, which were searching, searching on every side, commanded respect. It was curious to study how the smart city man's smile at the rustic faded into a look of serious, unfeigned interest as he caught sight of the old preacher's countenance.

"That is like war," he exclaimed at length, as the tents of the encampment started into view amid the trees and the flashes of the bay beyond. Approaching the gate, I asked the sentry:

"Can you tell us where we may find Major or Captain Parkridge, of the —th Vermont?" The

stiff guardsman rather overawed the elder. The
sentry made me, in fact, no reply, but turned his
face, rimmed by the patent-leather strap under his
chin, to the left, and spoke to the officer of the day.
This official stepped smartly towards us, and to
him I repeated my question.

"The —th Vermont? Why, that regiment has
gone back to the front; left Jersey City in the
other brigade yesterday. They were only here
for a day or two."

" To the front? It is too far," exclaimed the
elder, in absolute distress. "'Lish, before we can
get to him she will die !" He dropped his bag,
laid his umbrella against it, removed his tall hat,
and commenced rubbing his brows.

"You are distressed, sir," kindly rejoined the
lieutenant, as if he knew not what else to say, but
wished to offer some sympathy to the venerable
man.

"I want my boy. I'm a preacher. My wife
lies at the point of death, and I have come to get
my boy to go up on a furlough long enough to receive her parting blessing."

" What is his name? Is he an officer? If so,
you can undoubtedly reach him by telegram
easily enough."

"Horace Parkridge."

" Parkridge ?" exclaimed a brother officer, who
had been leisurely advancing down the company
street; and, indeed, two or three others made up
quite a group of officers about us in a few mo-

ments—"Parkridge? Why, that's the fellow with one arm."

"No; my boy Hod had two arms when he left home—no, that can't be the one," replied the elder, disposed to be relieved.

The officers smiled, yet a trace of pity was in their smiles as one of them ventured an explanation: "He may have had two good arms when he left home, my dear sir, but many things happen to us after we leave home in these days of battle you know."

"Elder," I interrupted, "it would be just like Horace to conceal a glorious deed by which he had lost an arm. He would be the last one to tell us of it, and especially to worry his mother with such tidings. I am sure that is the man we want," turning to the officer.

"Yes," responded the lieutenant, "the man is breveted major for his fine action when he lost his arm. I say—but you informed me that you were a clergyman. Step this way, you, friend of the minister," and he approached me. Then, in a by-talk, he asked: "Was the major always just right? I don't want to unnecessarily pain his father, but this Major Parkridge that I have in mind is down here on a furlough, and is—he's the best fellow in the world, as brave as a lion, but is a bit given to crooking his elbow, eh?"

"I'm afraid that is he," I replied, soberly.

"He was in camp here not more than an hour ago, and, I think, even then under the influence of liquor," replied the lieutenant. "You'll find him," and again he lowered his tone, "at Fore-kyte's. Do you know Forekyte's?"

"Of course I don't, sir."

"Exactly. You are from the country. So am I; but, unfortunately, since I have been stationed within reach of it, I have learned to know Fore-kyte's with many another unlucky officer. It is a place on —— Street, where army officers break over rules; but I doubt if you can get in there," and as he said this his voice was raised sufficiently for the elder to hear.

"What is that?" he demanded, eagerly. "Got trace of him? Got track of him? Know where he is and we can't get to him? I would like to see a place I couldn't follow my boy into—that is, in this world, I mean." And he replaced his hat, lifted his umbrella in one hand and his satchel in the other, wide apart, and then brought them together in front of him with a resounding whack.

"If you happen to have any bottles of medicine in that bag of yours, elder," laughed one of the lieutenants, "your collars and cuffs will smell of liniment after such another blow as that."

But the troubled gentleman was too serious for the slightest response to pleasantry. "Tell me —tell Mr. Elisha Stone, his life-long friend," he continued, "and me, his father, where is Captain, or Major, Horace Parkridge? There are no doors that can withstand us two if we put our shoulders against them."

But the reply was not forthcoming. After a brief consultation among the officers, in which I caught the words, " Only get his head broken—high-steppers, full of liquor and high play "—at length one of them gave us the direction to Fore-kyte's Hotel, and we started once more on our search. We wandered considerably, but at length we arrived in front of that once famous hostelry in —— Street, the elder remarking, as we stood gazing up into the great windows:

"Now, those arm-chairs up there behind that wide glass are full of blue-coats, and Horace would be mortified to death if I came in after him as if he were a truant school-boy. 'Lish, you go in, and tell him I'm out here waitin' for him."

" Mr. Parkridge," I replied, " we have reason to fear that your son has forgotten somewhat, temporarily, at least, his self-respect, or he would not be lounging around in a place of that dubious character. You may as well go in with me."

"It is dreadful to think on—my son, once so clean, so true, who would have put his duty before any play, and especially play in a place that brought a smirch upon his good name. It is the great city that does it, that ruins the boys, and yet it is not the city. A man ruins himself, wherever he is ruined. But I feel none the less as if I should drop to the earth, to think that those officers back there had to be ashamed to tell us where my boy was loungin' away his time

15

on a furlough. But come on. I will have him!" And he uttered the last with a tone of tremendous resolution, as if all his soul was rallied to the determination.

"Don't unnecessarily give yourself away now," I warned him. "You must not go in there with the purpose of preaching any sermon."

"Let go my sleeve," he answered. "It was only a moment ago that you were beggin' me to come, and now I am ready to go in. Let go! I need no caution. I know my duty. I will thunder the whole place down. I would like to take my stand by one of those billiard-tables and proclaim the everlasting—"

"Now, see here, elder, that won't do. You must go in quietly, say nothing to anybody except our boy, if we find him. If he is there we shall not have to wait for him; he will discover us almost as soon as we open the door, and he will come straight for us."

"Unless, oh, unless he is not himself. If I find him under the influence of the prince of the power of the air, I shall certainly bear my testimony against this Sodom and Gomorrah combined. It is no use to dissuade me, and you and I are not afraid of any Belials who snare young men to their ruin, if they march on us like the Amalekites in battle array."

"No, no, not afraid, but it will do no good your preaching in there." I had to pass these words over the good man's shoulder as he now pushed open the red leather doors before him and strode into the gaudy bar-room.

"Stand here a minute and look the landscape o'er," whispered the elder. "Here's more'n a hundred fair young men, most of them wearin' their country's shoulder-straps, wastin' their time guzzlin' liquors, and leanin' over them foolish tables, and lookin' on to see other fellows waste their time rollin' them balls about."

He went on in this vein of reflection and description of the place, which my own eyes could see for themselves, for a moment or two, when he was promptly interrupted by a waiter, who stepped in front of us swinging his hands and saying:

"Seats for refreshments in the next saloon, through the door, gentlemen."

"My young friend, see here," quickly responded the elder, bringing his huge hand down in a fatherly way on the waiter's shoulder; "see here, don't be in a hurry. I want to speak with you. We don't want any refreshments, and probably you don't want any of my moralizing. What we want, however, is my son, Captain, Major Horace Parkridge, of the —th Vermont Regiment, United States Volunteers. If you are the proprietor, or his son, now, perhaps, which is more likely, being so young evidently, you probably know Horace, for unfortunately he would be very familiar, and get acquainted with the proprietor of any tavern where he was stopping right off.

Everybody likes him, and he makes friends. Do you know him !"

"Your hand's heavy, old boy," protested the waiter, and his smile of derision had begun to give way to an angry growl through his white lips before the elder's explanation was half finished. "Let up on me, and go and get your drinks, if you want any."

"Old boy, do you say!" exclaimed the elder. "That's what you call a clergyman in New York, is it ?"

"Clergyman ! You are a clergyman, are you ? A clergyman from up country, I suppose. You object because I called you old boy ? Excuse me, but I would rather see the old boy than a minister. Let go of me. Let go of my shoulder !" he bawled out.

"Elder, see, every head in the room will be turned towards us in a moment. We must certainly avoid a disturbance. We don't want them all eying us."

"Yes, let 'em, let 'em look this way," he said, lifting his fine countenance, and raising his hat, "then I can see if the face that I love best is here among them all." The clear ringing voice that could sway a camp-meeting sounded like a trumpet-call through the rooms. Perhaps, after all, it was about as appropriate an assault as two unsophisticated persons like ourselves, and one of them a clergyman, could make on such a place. Perhaps there was more method in this mad naturalness of my companion than I at first supposed. At any rate, he made no attempt whatever to use any caution, but spoke and acted as he would in any assembly of our country village where he was universally revered. Unoccupied men pushed back their chairs and crowded towards us. The smoking spectators of the various billiard matches, who filled the long luxurious leather benches on either side of the room, saw the prospect of something more exciting than a lazy game between amateurs. They began to muster around us.

"Be careful, gentlemen. Remember the necessary quiet of a gentlemen's club, especially of army officers." It was the quick, sharp tones of the head-waiter, the major-domo, as he dropped down into the midst of us from somewhere. "What's the matter, Augustus?" addressing the waiter whom we had encountered first. "What's the country gentleman hanging on your shoulder for?"

"I let go promptly," the elder volunteered; "I just wanted to detain him for a moment as being a representative of the establishment, and I wanted to question somebody."

"Curse you!" growled the waiter called Augustus, squirming loose, and smoothing his ruffled linen over his shoulder, and then he flung another oath at the clergyman.

"Fined for that," promptly noted major-domo; "swearing at customers now," and he whipped out a note-book, on which he evidently recorded the incivility of the unfortunate Augustus.

"I'll lose my posish for the sake of swearing at that Yankee country priest," angrily continued Augustus, and he began to indulge again his profanity.

"Discharged," coolly added Mr. Major-domo, writing on another leaf of his book, which he tore off and thrust into Augustus's face.

"Why, then, I may as well punch him, too," yelled Augustus, livid with rage, as he sprang towards the elder.

"Oh, my poor deluded brother in Adam," exclaimed the elder, as he caught Augustus's wrist in that tremendous clasp of his brown and bony fingers. "No, 'Lish," he said, throwing the words to me, "I can manage him. All right, gentlemen. Heaven forgive the boy; he cannot hurt me," and Mr. Parkridge held the fellow in such a vise that the next moment he fairly yelled for mercy.

"Hurrah, hurrah, for the countryman!" burst from a dozen lips, most of whom had not understood the clerical character of my companion as yet.

"What in perdition is all this about?" That is the way I write it. Perdition was not the word used by the sleek proprietor, who, alarmed by the sound of the cheers, now pushed his swelling way in among us.

"I want my boy. Is this Mr. Forekyte? My

name is Parkridge, from Northbrook, Vermont.
I am a preacher. This is Mr. Elisha Stone, one
of my most respected neighbors, and the true and
loyal friend of my dear boy Hod. Hod, I am
afraid, sir, is stoppin' a few days at your tavern
here."

"My tavern! This is a rendezvous for army
officers, my friend. You are afraid, you say, that
your boy is a guest here. Afraid of what, reverend, sir?"

"Well, now, we will not discuss that. I will
skip the word, if you don't like it; and, if you
don't mind, without further interruption—for I
don't like attention over much—I'll commence to
stir round and see if I can't find Hod in some of
these rooms."

"No," replied Forekyte, stepping in front of
us, "you will neither discuss nor will you look
about. You will give us your room rather than
your company. That's what you'll do, my clerical friend. My guests don't come here for
preaching, nor to meet clergymen—who are all
well enough, I suppose, if they only keep in their
place." He said this with a broad grin flung out
over his flabby roll of neck fat at the crowd.
But, to his surprise, evidently his feeble attempts
at ridicule did not meet with a ready response
among the men who were standing amid his glitter, especially as they saw at nearer view the venerable white head in the centre of their muster.

"I will not inflict any more of an old father's

kind words on you, boys," the elder resumed, pathetically. His eyes ignored wholly the blustering Forekyte, but rested with a caressing gaze upon the group of officers now so close about him. Then he suddenly caught the nearest youthful captain by the arm, and asked, abruptly,

" You, now, my lad, where are you from? Where's your home?"

" From Maine, sir," answered the officer, with the utmost respect.

" And you, now?" grasping another, with the same blunt question.

" I'm from New Hampshire, elder?" answered the young fellow, who happened to be a lieutenant of the —th from that State.

" I thought so—up-country blood ; and I presume it is true with most of you. God bless you, boys, every one ! You look like good, sensible fellows enough, only you've got into a bad place in the great city. That's what your father would say up in Maine. And your mother on the granite hills, my lad, is probably thinking about sitting down when Saturday night's sun has sunk a little lower, and your father has brought in the milkin', and writin' you a dear good letter. Well, God bless her letter to you. Don't stay here, my dear children, I could almost call you."

" Now, see here, you venerable owl," bawled Forekyte, with savage interruption, quite forgetting his usual skill in managing his place, " you

can just step outside these doors and drop all the
tears you want; but you can't stay whining in
here, where men come to be happy and forget the
woes of life."

"Take that back, Forekyte, or I'll choke you
worse than your own fat neck!" It was a lieu-
tenant-colonel from Lamoile County, in our own
State, as I afterwards found out, who threw his
hot protest into the proprietor's face, as he pushed
his way in front of him menacingly.

At that moment a bell tinkled sharply, and instantly three or four burly fellows seemed to come
up out of the floor, or step from the wall, or drop
from the ceiling. I did not know from whence
they came, but there they were, advancing on us,
clubs in hand, though they did nor wear the uniform of policemen.

"Make way here," commanded one of these
men, just behind me.

"No you don't, my hearty," I answered him,
as I still kept in the way of his advance. "No
man must lay a finger on that harmless old gentleman while I live."

"You ox-driver," growled the fellow, in a low
tone, and lifted his club. I could not wait for the
club to descend, of course, that would not have
been prudent. I regret the blow that I gave him.
It was unnecessarily heavy. He was too much
swollen with beer-drinking to need so hard a blow
for doubling him together.

"'Lish, dear child," protested the elder, moving

towards me, his long arms parting the throng with a gesture such as one makes in swimming, "don't strike any one. God forbid. Push them one side, this way," and he renewed the swinging motion of his tremendous arms. "Remember that they that take the sword shall perish by the sword."

"But these are the clubs of rowdies, poor gentleman," exclaimed one of the officers. "There must, however, be no more of this violence, Forekyte. Come, boys, left dress and hollow square around the clergyman and his adjutant."

A dozen uniforms made such a solid wall about us in the next moment that Forekyte had an opportunity to collect his wits, as he saw the impossibility of reaching the disturbers. Smiling as if he would make the best of the situation, he cried:

"Hands off, all ; silence ! we'll have the patrol in here in a second more if you don't hush. Now, reverend gentleman, what is it that you really want? Excuse me. I·probably did not understand your errand. I don't want any sermons, but anything that you want, why, get it and go quietly, won't you ? I offer you my apology."

"I want," replied the elder, straightening up, as he still held my hand as a precautionary measure in his own ; he began in that same camp-meeting tone, clear and ringing : "I want my boy, Horace Parkridge. Is he here ? Horace, my dear son ?"

The voice was raised to its highest pitch, and

given its full compass. It echoed through the long rooms and up the brass-carpeted stairways, helped on by a hush to which all contributed, and which fell over not only those in our immediate apartment, but evidently far down the suite of rooms among the confusion of mirrors, "Horace, my dear son!"

Scarcely had the words left his lips before there came back : "Father!"

"There, at the head of the stairs," answered the elder, stretching out his arms over lesser men's heads, while a look, the like of which I have seen given to some colossal divinity in marble, gleamed in the old man's yearning face.

"Make way, gentlemen," some one cried, and the throng parted in a lane. As Horace descended the stairs his emotion sobered him somewhat and gave him the command of his footsteps. His tangled legs grew straighter by the instant as he dropped along down by the help of the banister, and when he touched the sawdust-sprinkled floor where we stood he walked erect, quickly advancing over the hundred feet or so that separated him from his father's embrace.

"God forgive me, father, what's the matter?" he cried, as he yielded his one hand. "And 'Lish!" and he moved the stump of an arm yet bandaged in an empty sleeve to indicate that he could not give me the other hand.

"Mother's dying, Hod!" and the elder, apparently oblivious of us all, at any rate with a naturalness which melted us all, bent down and kissed his son's scarlet forehead as if he had been a school-boy running into the home door-yard after a truancy.

"O God, have mercy on her and on me! Is there no time, no hope?" The broken voice, quavering with unspeakable emotion, the handsome face written over with such agony, the one hand left him put up on his father's shoulder, and the remnant of the other arm laid upon the preacher's broad breast and across his patriarchal beard of white, the wayward boy hid his face in his father's clasp. It was all done so quickly, and I think the crowd must have been made up of home-loving, home-sick, up-country soldiers, nearly every one; for the spectacle swept a tenderness over us like a bit of April weather, and every fellow's cheeks were wet in no time. There was not a click of a billiard-ball to be heard.

"By George!" I overheard the Lamoile County colonel say, as he moved by me to hide his emotion, "a fellow never has but one mother. I hope they'll get right off."

"Father, let's go at once."

"The three-o'clock New England," some one shouted out.

I record an actual fact. Forekyte himself touched a bell, and respectfully said: "There's a carriage at the door, reverend sir, at your disposal. You have an hour easily. But if you will—won't you eat something first?"

"No, father," protested Horace. "Thank you, Forekyte. Come, 'Lish, I have a month's furlough on account of this," holding up his arm. "There's no reason why we shouldn't get right off. Boys," turning to his brother officers, "I'll not forget any man who is in this crowd as soon as I get back to the army. If I can ever do you a service—"

"That's all right," they answered, in a score of voices.

"Don't waste any more time on us, major," urged some one.

"Hurrah for Major Parkridge, of the —th Vermont!" cried another. But there were no cheers.

"I would just like to say a word to you, boys," resumed the elder, one arm half around Horace's neck, and the other lifted as if he held blessings to shower on us as his closed fist was opened into five branching fingers. "'T'aint more 'n once in a lifetime that a preacher has such a chance as this. No doubt your chaplains give you lots of sermons." Some of the men smiled at this, I noticed. "But mine is like a loaf of brown-bread just baked in the old home oven. Now, listen to me, boys : get out of this. Excuse me, Mr. Proprietor, but you get out of this, too. Boys, you're away from home on an errand fit for angels. We're praying for you, night and morning and noon, up among the hills. May the power of the Most High have you all in his precious keeping ! If you were my own dear children, I couldn't

mean it more'n I do now. Come, let's shake
hands. Good-bye."

Reverently, with many a word of blessing,
man after man of that company came up and
grasped that old clergyman's extended palm.

"You're a good man, sir. If the world only
had more of such Christians we would all fall
in," said one.

"I'm not ashamed to ask you to remember me
in your prayers," said another, as he passed.
"But don't you think us all little devils ; we are
not so bad as we seem. We know a Christian
when we see him, which is not too often."

"Come, father," groaned Horace ; "you said
she was dying."

"Yes, yes, my son ; but she says she will live
until she sees you again. Yet we mustn't tempt
kind Providence by missing that train."

In the carriage Horace utterly broke down
with his sense of shame.

"You mustn't take on so," his father continually reassured him. "God is good. You can
be a man yet ; and Cynthia sent word— What
was it, 'Lish ?"

I began to tell the major the message that the
girl had sent, but he stopped his ears. Then he
begged me to go on again, and when I had finished my piecemeal narrative we were well on
towards the station. Weak with his wound, and,
I could also see, broken with the effect of some
days of evil-doing, he gave us deep solicitude by

the time the carriage stopped. I was not prepared, however, after I had returned with tickets, to hear him say calmly words which better befitted a mind unhinged:

"Father, take them my love—to my mother and to Cynthia. Ask them to forgive me—everybody in the old village—and forget me, for I cannot endure the shame. I cannot go home. My life must end at once on the battlefield, if I can by searching find an honorable death there."

We stood facing each other on the platform.

"'Lish "—with great solemnity the elder addressed me, and yet it had all the authority of a command ; he dropped again that gripsack to the platform, and laid his umbrella deliberately through the handle—"'Lish, grasp him !" and he once more swung those long arms, this time making a shackle about his son's body.

"Father, don't force me to resist you !" protested Horace.

"No ; you needn't resist if you don't want to," replied the elder. "But, resist or not, it don't make any difference, my boy; you're goin' home, if I can take you."

It would have been no less than a struggle amounting to assault if Horace had carried out his purpose to resist his father. He yielded. In fact, broken in spirit and in body, he was more like a child than a man. In a few minutes more the train was carrying us away towards the fond old hills of Yankeeland.

Of the soothing ministry which that good priest
of high heaven lavished upon his own son all the
journey through I cannot write—it would take an
inspired pen. It was old, yet ever new ; and there
is a power in the ancient faith that that good
man preached to cure a soul wounded to the
death. Of that I am sure. Of that this young
scapegrace stood a living proof.

CHAPTER XVII

It was the sunny afternoon of an Indian-summer day when we were met by Mary Holyoke in West Village. What a soft frame of mind Nature seems to fall into in a Vermont Indian summer of the late autumn!

"Is she yet living?" was the first question that fell from Horace's lips, and he was the first to speak.

"Yes; and may revive, the doctor says, if her mind can be brought to help her body. He is sure that there is something troubling her that has brought on this attack of prostration." It was the depot-keeper, good neighbor, who said this, significantly eying Horace.

The glory of that autumn air could not avail to stimulate our anxious hearts to further speech. For the most part we crawled up those rugged hill-sides in silence. An hour later Horace exclaimed again :

"Here are my feet once more on the old door-step, father. I am very thankful. Only your healing faith could have brought this all about. I never meant to have walked under the branches of these maples again."

16

The change that had come over him in self-possession, in calmness of spirit, and, indeed, in physical strength, was refreshing to us who had seen him prostrated in New York. He was still evidently suffering much pain from his arm.

"That is about the way some of the Virginia ruins look," continued Hod, pointing to the Bosworth place, from which a laggard wreath of smoke still occasionally arose from the conflagration of a few days before.

"Never mind, children," said Mr. Holyoke, hobbling along upon his staff to greet us; "there's good news afore you. You'll hev it yet, 'Lish; and you and Mary'll soon build a nest again among those ruins, if Polly Cark does her duty."

"Polly is here? — didn't run away, the wild creetur?" asked the elder.

"She's been here every hour since you left, faithfully at your wife's side."

"How do you do, Horace? Welcome home!" Cynthia said it as she stepped forward from the sitting-room.

"Cynthia Littlewood!" exclaimed Horace; and for a moment, as they grasped hands, they looked in each other's faces, and then he led her at once back into the sitting-room, closing the door behind him.

"Ah, well!" sighed the elder, as, with a blank look of disappointment, he saw his son depart through that door rather than the door into his mother's chamber, "young love ain't old love;

but he knows his mother is better, and after we
old folks are gone the young love may keep him
while the old is but a memory."

Then he threw off his own coat and walked into
the chamber of the invalid.

"Can we go in at once and see mother?" in-
quired Horace, reappearing but a few moments
later.

"It's all right, my dear, I guess," whispered
Mary Holyoke to the flushing Cynthia, as she
flew like a bird to her side. "Settled so soon
as that?"

"It must be all right, that which bid fair to
cause years of agony. We simply said, 'Forgive.' 'I forgive,'" was Cynthia's whispered reply. My heart gave a jump as I overheard it.

And then Mary's "So glad," as we all moved
towards the invalid's chamber.

"We mustn't all go in," I protested.

"Indeed we may," cried Mary; "she is going
to get well. Polly Cark has cured her; Polly
and your telegram from New York. These have
cured her."

"Polly Cark! What has she done?"

"Wait and see or hear. Remember, it is a
miracle, in a few days."

Horace opened the door. His mother was sitting up in the bed to receive him.

"Mother dear!"

"My dear child! God is good and true." And
the two were folded in each other's embrace.

Horace then knelt at the bedside; with her transparent hands on his dark hair, she said:

"O Saviour of mankind!"—her voice was so clear that we all wondered at its cadences—"save him ever, as thou hast thus far!"

I remember how the glory of the dying day fell through that west window-sash upon the white head and the brown, and the old clock that months before had struck a parting hour now struck the hour of greeting. Then, lifting herself up with astonishing strength, Mrs. Parkridge said:

"Polly, my own sister, bring your own daughter here. Let us give our own children our blessing."

I relate these astounding revelations, so abruptly made, in the exact order of their occurrence, and without any attempt at embellishment, for I am no artist. At that word Polly Cark ran to Cynthia, and as Cynthia put out her arms in surprise or defence against her assault, or yet, possibly, to prevent the little woman's sinking to the floor, Polly cried, with an exceeding pathos:

"My own child, Cynthia Cark!"

Cynthia did not speak; I believe she could not if she had tried.

"Horace, she will fall, too," I warned him. But the boy's one arm was of small avail to support the girl, and I was glad I had two good arms to help my old house-keeper to a chair. Cynthia, pale as none of us ever saw her, turned

to her lover and fell upon his shoulder in a pas-
sion of weeping, that refuge of women. I swow,
I thought she would cry herself to death! But
Hod held her hard, and said, at length,

"You have not kissed your mother." And
with that he led Cynthia over to Mrs. Cark's
chair.

"Are you indeed my mother?" asked the beautiful girl, still clinging to Horace's shoulder with
one hand, while she slowly put out the other till
at length it ventured to stroke the thin gray
locks of Polly's bowed head. "How strange,
when one has never had that filial love, to try
to awake it! If I cannot love you as I ought, my
mother, God help me, I will at least try," and she
stooped down to kiss Polly's brow. Still she
clung to her lover.

"Don't reprove her," the elder began ; "poor
Polly has suffered enough, God knows." The
man's tones trembled till he could hardly pour
the message from his heart.

"My dear," the elder continued, addressing his
wife, "can you endure more excitement? Shall
I explain to these young people?"

"Yes, yes, let us do right now. All this comes
from the worship of money, and from the mistaken rule of doing wrong that good might come
of it. And God will now forgive us." Mrs. Parkridge spoke with difficulty, and yet persisted, in
spite of her exhaustion, in finishing her comment.

"You see, children," the elder resumed, "when,

years ago, Samuel Cark, honest man, your father, Cynthia, failed to come back from a whaling voyage—he was lost at sea—we got Polly a place as house-keeper for the Senator. Mother was glad to do that for her own sister. Your birth took place under this roof of ours, and Polly left you here, Cynthia, a babe of a few weeks, to go work at the Senator's. That was the time the hard rich man was quarrelling with his last wife. Mrs. Bosworth's child was born then, and for a week or two the little new-comer seemed to have some hold on the hard old man, but he was too far crazed with dissipation, and the soul within him was eaten out by his high life, and he never was himself long. That baby died. Polly, poor soul—"

"Out of pity for the sick lady," exclaimed Polly. "She was sure that her baby was her only hold on her husband and her home. Make sure that was my first motive."

"Yes," resumed the elder, accepting the interruption, "out of pity, I believe, Polly came over and got you, Cynthia, her own baby, and put you in the poor lady's arms in place of the dead child."

"And when it was once done, it was done!" excitedly Polly shot the words out. "It was a lie; it was a crime. Oh, what falsehood we had to use! We buried the dead child secretly— just to think of it, going to the cemetery alone! But Mrs. Laura, that was the Senator's wife—was mistaken in her expectations. Nothing could control him long in those bad days, when he was going to pieces. In his next fury he expelled her into the night, and he insisted—oh, what a night of horrors it was!—that the baby, that is you, my precious child, should be bundled after its mother. As he said, 'Put it into the chest and take it after her!' I could not believe he meant it. I was sure Mrs. Bosworth would be recalled in a few days, with you."

"You were nearly crazed!" Mrs. Parkridge offered, in palliation, from her pillow.

"Yes; no one here knew what I had done till days had passed," resumed Polly, snatching at the narrative. "But that chest went out of the mansion with the lid propped, so that you could breathe, my baby; and once we were in the old shay I took you out and held you in my arms, and at the almshouse I gave you carefully into the nurse's arms, though I left the wooden chest. Peleg knows this much, for he drove the shay. I was tender and careful with my own baby that wicked night when I parted with her."

"And when we were informed," interrupted the elder, "you flew into such a state of mind relating it; we feared for your brain as you told to us what you had done, but we, too, burdened our souls with your secret, for which, perhaps, God has punished us. But we watched the child till Deacon Littlewood's wife adopted it. Indeed, we actually persuaded her to take it to her home. Then we were more at ease, because we thought of the deacon's wealth and Polly's poverty. May God forgive us if we thought too much of the money." And as his eyes rested upon Polly, he seemed giving utterance to her thoughts and plannings rather than his own, though he was too generous to charge it upon her.

"But I knew a lie would never prosper, and urged it day by day," whispered Mrs. Parkridge. "I knew it wasn't the way to do evil that good might come. I yielded for my own sister's sake, but only day by day, as it were. I feared the righteous Ruler of all things would have his way. Indeed, I ought to say, I hoped He would, and I claimed at least the right to defend my own son from getting into this cobweb of Satan."

"Which your righteous God overruled, mother dear," Horace could not help saying, with a fond glance into Cynthia's eyes. Then after a little of that silence, which the utmost astonishment often imposes, I ventured to ask:

"You, Polly Cark, told all this in exact truthfulness to the singer and Deacon Littlewood when you thought Cynthia was about to marry Felton?"

"Yes," she answered. "I wanted to prevent any more wrong being done—to you, in this instance."

"Oh, but they had gone too far," I remarked, thinking aloud.

"Certainly, and they are more guilty than yet appears," answered Mrs. Parkridge.

"You, Elisha Stone," the elder took up her sentence, "are Senator Bosworth's child, the child of the wife who followed him here from the South, and died at his gate. She was a creole from New Orleans."

As the silence of a deeper astonishment hushed us all once more, I thus took my place with Cynthia in that small company among earth's millions, who have the strangest of mortal experiences, the discovery of parents. I could not make any comment. I stood dumb !- The old Senator, then, was my father, the very relation which I once was so thankful was not mine.

"You are to thank Ashael Keep, the lawyer," resumed the elder, "for the full proof of all this. He came here almost as soon as Horace left for the war. Had it not been for mother's nerves— she said it would kill her to have all this old matter about Polly spread over the hill-sides among our neighbors—we should have told you what we were doing in the meanwhile."

"But I protested that I was ready to die, if need be, that my duty might be done," with some excitement Mrs. Parkridge urged it. "When you, dear Elisha, paid your money for the place, I should have spoken had I the proof that you were the proper heir. Then, however, I only had the bare idea. When the singer and Mr. Littlewood wronged you, and then when, later on, you were

hurt so in the woods, I said if you ever recovered
I would sell the clothing from my back, provided
we could not otherwise afford the expense, to fer-
ret out the proof of what I have now told you.
The wool money of this fall finally paid Ashael
Keep's expenses in his investigation. He went
West and hunted up the proof from the doctor's
son, whose dissipated life has since come to its
end. That Nashua doctor knew of the will—I
mean the Senator's aged brother."

At this juncture good Dr. Brown stole into the
room. With a quick eye he searched us all, from
the patient to the latest talkative intruder. With
uplifted hands he said :

"Now you must go out, all of you. Shoo, shoo!
She looks brighter. She will recover; but you
must be careful. Go out. Horace, how is this?"
and he took the arm which Cynthia was clinging
to, while he gave the half empty other sleeve a
professional tap of inquiry with his forefinger.

We obeyed the physician's injunction, while
Horace gave him some scanty narrative of the
brave deed by which he had lost his arm. As
soon as we were congregated in the great sitting-
room, and the doctor's inquiries were ended, I
said :

"Now, then, we must act with despatch. Send
for Keep. I do not care so much for my own
rights even—however gratefully I acknowledge
my debt to a kind overruling Providence that I
am likely to get my home again—as I care for

the punishment of that singer, who has caused us all so much suffering."

"It is nightfall of a wonderful day of mercy," protested the elder; "let us remember mercy to-day. To-morrow, wait till to-morrow. Justice will keep."

"Let's behave reverently," whispered Mary in my ear. "Come, put on your coat, Elisha Stone Bosworth, and let's you and I walk over by the twilight to see what we can do in the way of repairs to our home. We may need it soon," and she flushed the red roses of her cheeks to a brighter hue as she spoke it.

"No one hears you but me, and I have a right to hear it, Mary," I remarked, reassuring her modesty.

"You remember I was to speak next," she said, and with that two happier people never walked this dull earth than the pair that, with a hasty snatch at hats and outer garments from the pegs in the hallway, walked down that path by the well-sweep.

"You see, Mr. Bosworth," said Mary, dancing and tripping along at my side, "or I can see, that Major Parkridge must marry Cynthia Littlewood Cark—oh, how we have those names mixed up, have we not?—before he returns to the wars. They must have the house. You and I must move into our own, and that, too, very soon," pointing to the gray edifice, whose main outlines were preserved about in their original shape towards the east, notwithstanding the fire that had eaten away upon the other side.

"Why, you child," I replied, "there is nothing to hinder making a home next week. Shall it be next week?" And I got my answer in the old way of all humanity, too happy for words.

An hour later, as we wandered back to the Parkridge house, Mary exclaimed, "Why, there's Ashael Keep's gig!"

"That's akerit," asserted the little lawyer, stepping from behind the well-curb, where he had been taking a farewell whiff at his pipe, and he rapped it against the stone at the base of the curb, "an' you young folks wanter be married on this very evening o' November. If you ain't, it'll be a weddin' delayed."

"What?" we both of us exclaimed.

"About this. The deacon aforesaid has got out an indictment against you, Stone—pardon me, Mr. Bosworth—for breakin' an' enterin'. The sheriff 'll serve it early Monday mornin'. Better she's your wife, because you want to move right in and get settled and livin' happily afore you have any lawsuits to attend to. Then, too, there's that indictment against Felton for forgery," he began again, reading from a legal paper which he held in his hand. "But, what's the use?" he suddenly exclaimed, folding up the paper. "You don't care to hear all this legal lingo rehearsed. It's only for my own gratification, sort o' revengeful, I fear; I like to read it over.

I've been waitin' to fill up this blank so long, that now it's filled up by the Grand Jury I kinder like to read it over."

"But can we prove it?"

"You have that paper," he replied, with a slight twinkle in his eye.

"No," I answered. "It was lost in the fire."

"Are you sure? Wait and see. Cark's a shrewd one. But don't stan' here in the cold. Go in and stan' up before the minister and be married. What are you waitin' for?"

Within the next hour we had obeyed the lawyer's injunction. Our long waiting was over. It seems so strange that I should write the consummation of so many waiting hours in this single line. As we were receiving the greetings of the little home company, some one exclaimed,

"Now, Horace."

"Wait till we get through with Littlewood and Felton," put in the lawyer. "That'll be soon enough." And it was so agreed.

CHAPTER XVIII

"I LIKE it—everything!" exclaimed my wife, as we stood in the hallway of the old Bosworth house, surveying the effects of our ingenuity towards making the habitable parts homelike once more. We had been wedded three weeks now.

"Let me get that money from that Nashua estate and I am a rich man," I explained. "I shall be the only heir, the Chicago scapegrace of a son of the doctors' being dead."

"But I thought there was nothing in Nashua," observed Mary, her brown eyes lifted in wonder at my declaration that I was likely to be a rich man.

"True, it was supposed so. The land taken by the railroad, however, turns out to be very valuable. I shall get at least one hundred and fifty thousand dollars from that sale." ·

"Oh, wonder of wonders!" She clapped her hands and flew in to get ready for our drive to the village. The colt was even then standing at the door behind me. As she reappeared her first word was,

"Now, you must let me do what my heart prompts me, you rich man, Mr. Bosworth."

"What is that?" I asked, as I helped her in
behind my dear Skip, with which this story took
its first ride.

"Let's pay Cynthia twice what this furniture
cost her."

"Agreed. Go, Skip."

" And more," she pursued, as we spun down the
highway. "Let's be munificent. Father and mother,
of course, get our home back from Mr. Littlewood."

" Yes; he has begged to be allowed ' in the
Lord's marcy, brethering,' to count that whole
business as a great mistake, and has receipted
your father's debt."

" Well, why not sell all the land below the hill,
just keeping the house, our old home, for father
and mother, and give to Cynthia the product of
the sale?"

" Is that business?"

" Indeed it is not, you selfish. Don't you now
fall into the greed of gain that has been the destruction of so many others, just because you have
so much."

"Well, God help me," I responded, with genuine feeling, "it shall be as you wish. Besides,
Cynthia, now being cast off by Littlewood, really
has nothing."

" And Horace has nothing except the elder's
farm," Mary resumed. " He thinks he can hardly marry yet. I got this out of Cynthia. Horace
is talking about what he will possibly save from
his army pay."

"But if we get this singer, Felton, into prison or the Legislature, Horace can go back as colonel. Governor Trimbull assures the elder that he will commission Horace colonel as certain as Felton is out of the way."

" Oh, dear, dear," sighed Mary, as we rose and fell along the glorious drive, and such happiness was in our hearts, " I do wish that Horace did not need to go back to the war."

"I don't agree with you," I answered. "In fact, I rather think I ought to go myself."

" You !"

" Why not ?" And my bride of three weeks did not reply.

" Do you know where we are going now?" I asked at length, to break in upon her silence.

" You are going to that town-meeting, are you not ?" she asked. " Oh, suppose they elect you to Montpelier ?"

I smiled in spite of myself, but answered : " It wouldn't make Felton laugh if he were disappointed in his eagerly - sought - for election now, would it ?"

" He is a candidate ?"

" Yes; that is why he has returned at this time from the army—that and his anxiety about the Bosworth place."

" Yes," Mary resumed ; "and I suppose he thinks he has placated all the country-side by his boastful surrender of your estate. That card of his, now, in the *Saturday Evening Gazette*, setting forth that it was all a most unfortunate error, and all that."

"But Ashael Keep has a blow for him."

"What is that?" she asked.

"Now, your woman's curiosity must wait," I answered.

A little later, leaving Mary at the union store for some shopping, I soon found myself in the town-hall, that same room where this narrative began a little over a year previous. The assembled farmers were gathered in excited knots, discussing the candidacy of various persons.

As the moderator had not yet called the meeting to order, it was proposed to have a speech from Colonel Arthur Alfred Felton, the foremost candidate for town representative; that is, if you could reckon what he had said of himself in his abundantly displayed hand-bills.

"A speech, a speech," rang through the hall. Felton was ready, and rose to reply. He never made a finer appearance in all his life than he did standing there before his fellow-townsmen.

"That is just where he stood about a year ago now, 'Lish," whispered Horace, as he came up behind me, and surprised me with a touch of my elbow.

"Here's our hero. Hurrah! Hurrah! for Major Parkridge, the wounded soldier." The boy had scarcely crossed the threshold and shown his face before this hearty greeting met him, and it was

17

entirely spontaneous, in striking contrast with
Felton's wire-pulling cheers.

"He don't like it, Elisha, does he?" said Horace, as the cheers rose for himself. "See him
struggle to hide his anger under that handsome
face."

"Fellow-citizens." The words had hardly fall-
en from the colonel's lips in that clear, persua-
sive tone, of which I have often spoken, before he
had compelled the listening of us all. Men were
always charmed when he spoke. The honest
towns-people seemed to forget their prejudices
and their scruples; and, besides all that, have I not
uniformly confessed that he was a handsome fellow, engaging, and of fine speaking ability?

Into the midst of his first five minutes of glowing address Ashael Keep and the sheriff wedged
their way as an iron wedge is sometimes driven
into a maple log. Keep finally stepped upon the
platform, and drew near enough to put out his
hand and touch the orator upon the shoulder.
I happen to know just what the whispered words
were that fell into the speaker's ear.

"Felton," said Keep, "we have that forged
deed. Polly Cark preserved it."

Quicker than any word can describe it the
colonel turned and said, "You lie, you little dried-
up lawyer!"

Instantly the hush of expectation fell upon the
assembled countrymen, notwithstanding the momentary commotion of movement towards the

platform. Such words were not common in our quiet political meetings.

"That's a serious charge, townsmen," whined little Ashael, a quiet smile of conscious power working over his face. "This man's a forger, and I can prove it."

"That's so, br—feller-citizens," cried Deacon Littlewood, who, from some surprising conceal-ment, began to push his way towards the plat-form. "My conscience won't let me keep com-pany wi' this son o' Belial any more; I'm too much a lover o' righteousness. Keep's got th' forger in his fingers."

Felton turned pale as marble, but glanced a moment at the fatal paper, then at his white-haired partner in the game, thus turned State's evidence, then his dark eyes wandered in almost pitiable search over the sea of faces until they rested on Horace and myself, when they flashed a fire of defiance.

"Come, get your bail," commanded the sheriff, as Felton did not offer to move.

"I will, and I'll return," he said, confidently, as he stepped down from the platform to accompany the lawyer and the officer out of the room.

Why should I dwell upon the picture? He never did return. When he had served out his five years in the State's prison Arthur Alfred Felton went to South America. It is said he ac-cumulated a fortune there.

Within an hour of the time when Felton left

the hall, by one of those strange and popular movements that no one can explain, I was elected the representative to Montpelier in his place. That was the beginning of my political career, which has never taken me higher than lieutenant-governor of my own State.

Horace and Cynthia were married on Christmas day. By the beginning of the new year he was back again at the front, where he served in honorable position, using a brigadier-general's sword eventually with his one arm. He has valued politics higher than I, and is now a representative at Washington. I hope that he may eventually sit in my father's seat in the Senate. Mrs. Parkridge recovered from the illness that bore her so near to the grave, and only a year ago this writing passed on with her beloved husband, the two almost joining hands for the transit across the dark river. Even as I write I can look from my library window over the russet fields to the marble headstone which marks the spot where this venerable couple sleep beside my own mother's.

Polly Cark lives on. Her great age does not dim the dark eyes that gleam yet with some of their old fire. But the peace of her present life has made her gentle in her daughter's home. And, I am glad to record, there is no one she loves better than my own oldest daughter, who often acts as the staff of her tottering feet, for she cherishes only good-will to mine and me.

Of Mr. Littlewood it is enough to say that he is himself even in his age; and as he is now alone in the world, the sole occupant of his solitary farm-house and his own companion, that is punishment enough.

So now, the afternoon sun being low down towards the mountains, let the twilight fall. The countryman's story is told. It is our home muster hour. Let the night thicken later, for we have shelter under the protection of the good God, who has had his own way in our lives, as He always does with all in this world. I have nothing to dread when the next day's sunrise breaks in upon Bosworth House.

THE END.

By MARY E. WILKINS.

PEMBROKE. A Novel. Illustrated. 16mo, Cloth, Ornamental, $1 50.

JANE FIELD. A Novel. Illustrated. 16mo, Cloth, Ornamental, $1 25.

YOUNG LUCRETIA, and Other Stories. Illustrated. Post 8vo, Cloth, Ornamental, $1 25.

A NEW ENGLAND NUN, and Other Stories. 16mo, Cloth, Ornamental, $1 25.

A HUMBLE ROMANCE, and Other Stories. 16mo, Cloth, Ornamental, $1 25.

GILES COREY, YEOMAN. Illustrated. 32mo, Cloth, Ornamental, 50 cents.

We have long admired Miss Wilkins as one of the most powerful, original, and profound writers of America; but we are bound to say that "Pembroke" is entitled to a higher distinction than the critics have awarded to Miss Wilkins's earlier productions. As a picture of New England life and character, as a story of such surpassing interest that he who begins is compelled to finish it, as a work of art without a fault or a deficiency, we cannot see how it could possibly be improved.—*N. Y. Sun.*

The simplicity, purity, and quaintness of these stories set them apart in a niche of distinction where they have no rivals. —*Literary World*, Boston.

Nowhere are there to be found such faithful, delicately drawn, sympathetic, tenderly humorous pictures.—*N. Y. Tribune.*

The charm of Miss Wilkins's stories is in her intimate acquaintance and comprehension of humble life, and the sweet human interest she feels and makes her readers partake of, in the simple, common, homely people she draws.—*Springfield Republican.*

PUBLISHED BY HARPER & BROTHERS, NEW YORK.

By CHARLES DUDLEY WARNER

THE GOLDEN HOUSE. Illustrated by W. T. SMED-
LEY. Post 8vo, Ornamental Half Leather, Uncut Edges and Gilt Top, $2 00.

It is a strong, individual, and very serious consideration
of life; much more serious, much deeper in thought, than the
New York novel is wont to be. It is worthy of companion-
ship with its predecessor, "A Little Journey in the World,"
and keeps Mr. Warner well in the front rank of philosophic
students of the tendencies of our civilization.—*Springfield Republican.*

A LITTLE JOURNEY IN THE WORLD. A Novel.
Post 8vo, Half Leather, Uncut Edges and Gilt
Top, $1 50; Paper, 75 cents.

THEIR PILGRIMAGE. Illustrated by C. S. REIN-
HART. Post 8vo, Half Leather, Uncut Edges
and Gilt Top, $2 00.

STUDIES IN THE SOUTH AND WEST, with Comments
on Canada. Post 8vo, Half Leather, Uncut
Edges and Gilt Top, $1 75.

OUR ITALY. Illustrated. 8vo, Cloth, Ornamental,
Uncut Edges and Gilt Top, $2 50.

AS WE GO. With Portrait and Illustrations.
16mo, Cloth, Ornamental, $1 00. ("Harper's
American Essayists.")

AS WE WERE SAYING. With Portrait and Illustrations. 16mo, Cloth, Ornamental, $1 00.
("Harper's American Essayists.")

THE WORK OF WASHINGTON IRVING. With Por-
traits. 32mo, Cloth, Ornamental, 50 cents.

PUBLISHED BY HARPER & BROTHERS, NEW YORK.

☞ *The above works are for sale by all booksellers, or will be
sent by the publishers by mail, postage prepaid, to any part of the
United States, Canada, or Mexico, on receipt of the price.*

By BRANDER MATTHEWS

VIGNETTES OF MANHATTAN. Illustrated by W. T.
SMEDLEY. Post 8vo, Cloth, Ornamental, $1 50.

In "Vignettes of Manhattan" Mr. Matthews renders
twelve impressions of New York with admirable clearness
and much grace. From the collection a vivid picture may be
drawn of the great city.—*N. Y. Evening Post.*

AMERICANISMS AND BRITICISMS, with Other Essays
on Other Isms. With Portrait. 16mo, Cloth,
Ornamental, $1 00.

A racy, delightful little book. . . . It is a long time
since we have met with such a combination of keen yet fair
criticism, genuine wit, and literary grace.—*Congregationalist,*
Boston.

THE STORY OF A STORY, and Other Stories. Illustrated. 16mo, Cloth, Ornamental, $1 25.

STUDIES OF THE STAGE. With Portrait. 16mo,
Cloth, Ornamental, $1 00.

THE ROYAL MARINE. An Idyl of Narragansett
Pier. Illustrated. 32mo, Cloth, Ornamental,
$1 00.

THIS PICTURE AND THAT. A Comedy. Illustrated. 32mo, Cloth, Ornamental, 50 cents.

THE DECISION OF THE COURT. A Comedy. Illustrated. 32mo, Cloth, Ornamental, 50 cents.

IN THE VESTIBULE LIMITED. A Story. Illustrated. 12mo, Cloth, Ornamental, 50 cents.

PUBLISHED BY HARPER & BROTHERS, NEW YORK.

☞ *The above works are for sale by all booksellers, or will be sent
by the publishers by mail, postage prepaid, to any part of the United
States, Canada, or Mexico, on receipt of the price.*

By GEORGE DU MAURIER

TRILBY. A Novel. Illustrated by the Author. Post
8vo, Cloth, Ornamental, $1 75.

It is a charming story told with exquisite grace and tenderness.—
N. Y. Tribune.

"Trilby" is the best fiction of the older school that the magazines
have permitted the public to enjoy for a long while.—*N. Y. Evening Post.*

Proves Du Maurier to have as great power as George Meredith in
describing the anomalies and romances of modern English life; while
his style is far more clear and simple, and his gift of illustration adds
what few authors can afford. Thackeray had this artistic skill in some
degree, but not to compare with Du Maurier.—*Springfield Republican.*

"Trilby" is so thoroughly human, so free from morbidness and
the disposition to touch the unclean thing that it atones for a multi-
tude of sins in contemporaneous fiction. . . . In giving this wholesome,
fascinating history to the world the artist-author has done a favor to
novel readers which they cannot well repay nor fitly express.—*Indian-
apolis Journal.*

PETER IBBETSON. With an Introduction by his
Cousin, Lady * * * * * ("Madge Plunket"). Edited
and illustrated by GEORGE DU MAURIER. Post 8vo,
Cloth, Ornamental, $1 50.

Mr. Du Maurier deserves the gratitude of all who come across his
book, both for the pleasant and tender fancies in which it abounds
and for its fourscore dainty sketches.—*Athenæum,* London.

There are no suggestions of mediocrity. The pathos is true, the
irony delicate, the satire severe when its subject is unworthy, the comedy sparkling, and the tragedy, as we have said, inevitable. One or
two more such books, and the fame of the artist would be dim beside
that of the novelist.—*N. Y. Evening Post.*

The personal characterization is particularly strong, the pictures
of Paris are wonderfully graphic, and the tale will induce many of its
readers to attempt Du Maurier's receipt for "dreaming true."—*Phil-
adelphia Ledger.*

Novelty of subject and of treatment, literary interest, pictorial
skill—the reader must be fastidious whom none of these can allure.—
Chicago Tribune.

PUBLISHED BY HARPER & BROTHERS, NEW YORK.

☞ *The above works are for sale by all booksellers, or will be sent by
the publishers, postage prepaid, to any part of the United States, Canada, or
Mexico, on receipt of price.*

HARPER'S AMERICAN ESSAYISTS

Each volume contains a Portrait of the Author.

16mo, Cloth. $1 00 each.

PUBLISHED BY HARPER & BROTHERS, NEW YORK.

☞ The above works are for sale by all booksellers, or will be sent by the publishers by mail, postage prepaid, to any part of the United States, Canada, or Mexico, on receipt of the price.